"You really do want us to just be friends."

"It's not what I want," she admitted, "but I think it's the most sensible solution."

She couldn't tell what he was thinking. Did it matter? She'd long learned the only person who was going to take care of her was her.

"It's your call," he said. "We can be just friends. But I refuse to forget what happened."

She was torn in two. Part of her applauded her rational, mature decision. The other part snorted in disgust and warned her she would be very sorry to be sleeping alone tonight.

"I won't forget, either," she told him, and meant it.

Dear Reader,

There's something wonderful and magical about falling in love, but family complications can really get in the way. Why is it the people we love most in the world are also the ones who make things the most difficult? Sometimes without even trying.

In Crissy's case, the family in question is the amazing couple who adopted the baby she gave up. Twelve years after the fact, she really wants contact with her son. Which seems simple enough, but, of course, it isn't simple at all. Then there's the falling in love part. Talk about the right guy at the wrong time...and in the wrong place!

I love writing about families and friends. *Her Last First Date* gave me the chance to explore the best of both worlds. If you read the first two books in the POSITIVELY PREGNANT series, you'll have a chance to catch up with old friends. If you're new to the series—welcome. *Her Last First Date* will stand on its own.

Enjoy and happy reading!

Susan Mallery

SUSAN MALLERY

HER LAST FIRST DATE

Silhouette

SPECIAL EDITION®

Published by Silhouette Books

America's Publisher of Contemporary Romance

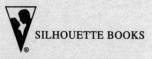 SILHOUETTE BOOKS

ISBN-13: 978-0-373-24831-5
ISBN-10:   0-373-24831-8

HER LAST FIRST DATE

Visit Silhouette Books at www.eHarlequin.com

Printed in U.S.A.

Books by Susan Mallery in miniseries

Silhouette Special Edition

Hometown Heartbreakers

The Best Bride #933
Marriage on Demand #939
Father in Training #969
Part-Time Wife #1027
Holly and Mistletoe #1071
Husband by the Hour #1099
Good Husband Material #1501
Completely Smitten #1520
One in a Million #1543
Quinn's Woman #1557

Lone Star Canyon

The Rancher Next Door #1358
Unexpectedly Expecting #1370
Wife in Disguise #1383

Positively Pregnant

Having Her Boss's Baby #1759
The Ladies' Man #1778
Her Last First Date #1831

Triple Trouble

The Girl of His Dreams #1118
The Secret Wife #1123
The Mysterious Stranger #1130

Bride of Bradley House

Dream Bride #1231
Dream Groom #1244

Desert Rogues

*The Sheik's
   Kidnapped Bride* #1316
*The Sheik's
   Arranged Marriage* #1324
*The Sheik's
   Secret Bride* #1331
*The Sheik and
   the Runaway Princess* #1430
*The Sheik and
   the Virgin Princess* #1453
*The Prince and
   the Pregnant Princess* #1473
*The Sheik and
   the Princess in Waiting* #1606
*The Sheik and
   the Princess Bride* #1647
*The Sheik and
   the Bride Who Said No* #1666
*The Sheik and
   the Virgin Secretary* #1723

Silhouette Desire

The Million Dollar Catch

The Substitute Millionaire #1760
The Unexpected Millionaire #1767
The Ultimate Millionaire #1772

SUSAN MALLERY

is a *USA TODAY* bestselling author of over eighty romances. Her combination of humor, emotion and just-plain-sexy has made her a reader favorite. Susan makes her home in Washington State, where the whole rain thing is highly exaggerated and there's plenty of coffee to help her meet her deadlines. Visit her Web site at www.SusanMallery.com.

Chapter One

Crissy Phillips believed in chocolate as a cure for heartache, exercise as a cure for everything else and second chances...for everyone but herself. Which was why she'd been standing outside the Kumquat Diner for the past fifteen minutes, instead of going inside for her meeting. Going inside was too much like forgiving herself and Crissy wasn't ready to do that just yet.

She knew all the arguments. She'd been young. She'd made the best choice she could at the time. If a friend of hers were in the same position, Crissy would cheerfully tell her to get over it and move on. Why was it always so much easier to give advice to other people, than to herself? Why did everyone else's life look so easily fixable, while elements of her own seemed an unfathomable mess? Why was she talking to herself in the middle of a diner parking lot?

She took a single step toward the front door of the diner, then stopped.

Just do it, she told herself. Do it, do it, do it.

When the chanting didn't work, she tossed her head and felt the light brush of her newly clipped hair on the back of her neck. She'd spent over two hundred dollars on red and gold highlights and an impossibly up-to-the-minute cut that actually suited her face. Didn't she want to flaunt her new and improved self?

She hated being indecisive and insecure. She was a successful businesswoman, a take-charge person. She made decisions easily and except for being an absolute failure when it came to her knitting class, she kicked butt wherever she went.

Not literally, of course.

It was one meeting. How scary could that be? She really needed to—

The front door of the diner opened and a tall, good-looking guy stepped out. He had reddish-brown hair, surprisingly close to her own untouched color, and eyes that belonged on a billboard on Sunset Strip, the color of moss after rain, framed by big, thick lashes. Crissy didn't consider herself a very sentimental person, but she was thinking an ode or two to those eyes might very well be in order.

"Hi," he said with a smile. "Are you the one I've been waiting for?"

It was an opening line that deserved a movie score,

she thought as she grinned. "You forgot 'all my life.' For that question to really work, you need the tag line."

His smile widened, then he glanced at his watch. "More like for the past ten minutes. Are you Crissy?"

She hadn't had to meet the devil head-on. He'd come to find her. Although Josh Daniels wasn't really the devil. He was a kind man who'd offered to help, at his brother's suggestion. Actually, the word "facilitate" had been tossed around, but Crissy could never use that word in a sentence without fighting a fit of giggling.

"Hi, Josh," she said. "Nice to meet you."

He raised his eyebrows. "I'm not sure nice covers it. You've been standing out here, trying to decide if you should come in for the past ten minutes. So is it me or the circumstances that have you dancing in the parking lot?"

"I wasn't dancing," she said primly, trying to ignore the fact that he'd obviously seen her and guessed she was slightly ambivalent about their meeting. "I was getting in touch with my inner…"

"Self?" he offered.

While weak, it worked. "Right," she said.

"Are you in touch now?" he asked.

As much as she was going to be. "I'm fine."

"Good." He pulled open the door. "I got us a booth. It has a great view of the parking lot. You'll like it. Come on, this won't be so bad."

As she'd requested the meeting, she had little choice except to follow him into the brightly lit interior. He led the way to a booth in the back which, unfortunately, did offer a clear view of the parking lot.

"So you witnessed my mental moment," she said

as she slid onto the bench seat. "How comforting. Having exposed myself at my worst, I have only one direction to go."

He settled across from her. "If that's your worst, you're a lot better off than most people." He leaned back and studied her. "Let's admit the situation is un- usual and awkward. So we'll take it slow. Talk about regular stuff for a while. How does that sound?"

"Good," she admitted. "You're being really nice about all of this."

"I'm a really nice guy. Incredibly intelligent and gifted…but let's not talk about me."

She grinned. "How refreshing to meet a man who knows his place in the universe."

The waitress appeared with two menus. Both Crissy and Josh ordered coffee. When they were alone, Crissy said, "Thanks for agreeing to meet with me. Pete and Abbey have always been so open and inviting. I just never felt right about…"

She stopped and pressed her lips together. No. She was going to tell the truth, even though it wasn't pretty and didn't reflect well on her.

"Until recently, Brandon has been more theory to me than the actual child I gave up for adoption," she ad- mitted. "Every time Abbey sent me a note or called, I never knew what to say. It was easier to stay away."

The waitress returned with two mugs of coffee, then left.

"I'm not here to make trouble," Crissy added. "I just thought it might be nice if I could meet him or some- thing."

She wondered if Josh would make a crack about her turning thirty and finally hearing the first not-so-subtle ticks of her biological clock, or if he would be defensive. Instead he simply regarded her thoughtfully with his soulful green eyes, saying nothing.

"What are you thinking?" she asked after a few minutes of silence.

"That you've spent a lot of time beating yourself up about giving up a baby for adoption. You were what—seventeen?"

When she got pregnant, but eighteen when he was born. "I'd finished high school," she said, not sure if she was explaining or trying to manipulate him into yelling at her.

Because he was right. She did beat herself up a lot. She'd taken the easy way out—she'd chosen to have the life she'd planned instead of raising her child herself. No matter how she rearranged the facts, she couldn't seem to make herself the honorable party.

Josh continued to study her. "Abbey can't have kids. She told you, right?"

Crissy nodded. "The first time we met. She'd had an accident when she was younger and the result was she couldn't have children. She and Pete started looking into adoption as soon as they got married. My parents knew their lawyer and on their first anniversary, we met to talk about them taking Brandon."

She didn't remember much about that meeting except Pete and Abbey had both been incredibly nice and understanding. She'd instantly felt comfortable with the young couple and knew they were the ones. But she hadn't been willing to be a part of their family, no matter how many invitations they issued. She couldn't allow herself—it was her punishment.

"Here's how I look at it," Josh said. "Pete and Abbey both want tons of kids. You gave them their first. Why would I think that was anything but totally cool?"

Despite the rush of emotion she had flowing through her body at the moment, she smiled. "Totally cool?"

He grinned. "You can pick another phrase if you want."

"No, that one works." She reached for her napkin and began to pleat it. "Okay, here's another question. Why are they being so nice about this? It's been nearly thirteen years. After all this time, I finally want to meet Brandon. Aren't they scared I'm going to do something horrible? Like take him back or try to become the most important person in his life?"

"Are you?"

"No, but they don't know that."

He sipped his coffee. "Yeah, they do."

Because they were nice, Crissy thought, again remembering that first meeting with the couple. While she appreciated nice, in these circumstances, she wasn't sure she trusted it.

"I want to meet Brandon." She said the words for the first time in her life. She'd e-mailed them to Abbey, but she'd never actually said them aloud before. "I want to get to know him. But not in an intense way. Something easy and casual."

"That can be arranged."

"I'm not prepared to tell him who I am," Crissy continued. That decision was a whole lot more about Brandon than her. While he knew he was adopted and had a birth mother somewhere in the world, knowing and meeting were two different propositions. He was only a kid. They should get to know each other before getting into issues.

"Abbey told me how you felt and why. We all agree with your logic." He leaned toward her. "Crissy, it's okay. Pete and Abbey have been hoping you'd want to get to know Brandon. They feel having his birth mother in his life will give him a connection with his heritage."

"His heritage? Great. Now I feel like a building."

Josh chuckled. It was a low, warm sound that eased her tension.

"You don't look anything like a building. Trust me," he said.

The funny part was, she wanted to. There was something about Josh Daniels that made her think maybe, just maybe, everything was going to work out.

"I have this nagging sense of punishment," she said, without meaning to say that aloud. "That I should be, or will be."

"Because you want to meet the child you gave up for adoption?"

"Sort of." The feeling was more vague than that. More impending doom than actual event. "Like I don't deserve a second chance when it comes to this."

Josh studied her. "I'm not a psychologist," he began.

Despite everything, Crissy smiled. "Oh, no. That statement is usually followed by the word 'but' and some advice or opinion."

"You think you know everything."

"I actually know a lot."

He sipped his coffee. "I'm not a professional, but…"

"See?"

He ignored her. "But it seems to me the only person intent on judging and punishing is you. Maybe it's time to move on."

Sensible advice. Advice she should take.

"So who are you?" she asked. "I know you're Pete's brother, but what do you do with your day?"

"I'm a doctor. Pediatric oncologist."

It took a second for her to make the connection. "Kids with cancer?"

He nodded. "I take the tough cases—the ones no one else will deal with. I spend my day searching for miracles."

She'd thought Pete and Abbey were too good to be true. Apparently it was a family trait.

"That has to be hard," she said.

He shrugged. "The success rates aren't as high as any of us would like, but I'm determined to give those kids and their families hope. Sometimes hope is all they have."

There was compassion in his expression and his voice, which probably explained why it was so easy for him not to worry about what she'd done. In his world, giving away a healthy baby to a loving couple delighted to start their family wasn't even a blip on the radar screen.

Maybe she should look at her situation from his perspective.

Crissy wasn't what Josh had expected. Intellectually he'd known she had to be close to thirty, but in his mind, he'd half expected a frightened teenager to show up. But if Brandon had grown from a baby to a happy, athletic twelve-year-old it made sense his birth mother had also changed.

He knew the basics about Crissy—that she came from a good family, had a college education, wasn't married and that she deposited money into Brandon's college fund every year on his birthday. Although Pete and Abbey had encouraged her to become a part of the family, she'd never been willing to take that step. Until now.

He'd always thought of her as "the birth mother." Never as her own person. Until meeting her, he'd never considered that there was someone in the world who had Brandon's eyes or his smile.

"I see you in him," he said.

"In a good way or a bad way?"

"A good way."

She smiled and while he was reminded of his nephew, he also saw Crissy. She was pretty, with short, shiny hair and big eyes. There was something about the way she moved, something sensual and…

He slammed on the mental brakes and backtracked. Sensual? Since when did he notice things like that?

"Abbey says he's really good at sports," Crissy said. "His dad played football in high school and ran track. I went out for nearly every sport I could. I went to college on a softball scholarship. I thought I was tough."

He grinned. "I'm sure you were."

"Does that intimidate you?"

"I'm shaking so hard, I can't stand."

"I don't believe that, but thanks for pretending."

"Abbey mentioned you own your own business. I don't think she told me what it was."

"Gyms for women. I have six now. They're all over this area."

"Impressive."

It explained the body he'd noticed when she'd walked in. She wasn't tall, but she looked fit, with curves in all the right places. He eyed her sweater and had a sudden desire to see her in tight workout clothes.

Which meant what? After four years of being alone, he was finally coming back to life?

Pete had spent the past two years bugging him to start dating, to get out and have fun. Josh had hidden behind his impossible work schedule. The thought of getting involved still seemed unfeasible, but maybe something casual wasn't out of the question.

"Are you ready to take the next step with Brandon?" he asked Crissy.

She shivered. "No, but I'll never be ready. I think I just have to leap in and hope for the best."

"Pete and Abbey just got word that their adoption of their new baby, Hope, is final. There's going to be a big party to celebrate. Lots of friends and family. You could blend in with the crowd."

Crissy swallowed. "That sounds like a plan. When's the party?"

"Saturday at three."

She pressed a hand to her chest. "I may start hyperventilating. Does one bring a present to an adoption party?"

"It's not required."

"But if I want to?"

"Abbey's registered at a baby store." He gave her the name.

Crissy's expression turned wistful. "I love baby stuff. Those little dresses and frilly socks. They're so cute. Probably not to you."

"Not really my thing."

"So what is your thing? What do you do for fun?"

Interesting question. Four years ago, he'd had a list. He and Stacey, his late wife, had enjoyed anything outdoors, when her health permitted. She'd loved cooking and gardening. They'd also been studying Italian together, in anticipation of a trip to Venice they never got to make.

"Work keeps me busy," he said. "What about you?"

"A lot of work, too," she said. "Running a business is always a challenge, but I like it. Living out here in Riverside means we're close to a lot of outdoor stuff. I hike a lot in the mountains, and I ski in the winter. Downhill and cross country. I'm a hideous knitter, but I keep trying because my friends love it. But I'm so awful, I had to give the owner of the store a free membership to one of my gyms just to stay in the class."

He laughed.

"I'm not kidding," she protested. "I swear, I have the antiknitting gene. Yarn hates me. I've seen a petition going around the shelves. If enough yarn signs, I'll be forced to stop taking classes."

He liked her. He knew that's what Abbey would ask first. If he'd liked her.

Crissy drew in a breath. "Okay, so we're set, right?

I'm coming to the party on Saturday. You're sure it's okay? No one will mind?"

He reached across the table and put his hand on hers. He'd meant the gesture as one of comfort and was surprised to feel an almost electric jolt of energy jump between them.

"You'll be fine," he said, ignoring the sensation and removing his hand more quickly than he'd planned.

"You don't actually know that. I suppose what with you being a doctor and all, you think you have a edge on stating that opinion, but you can't be totally sure."

He grinned. "Deep breaths."

"Not going to help."

She collected her purse and stood. He rose as well and tossed five dollars on the table to cover the coffee and tip.

"I'll be there," she said. "At three. Maybe ten after. Give other people time to arrive."

He pulled a business card out of his wallet, then wrote on the back. "My cell number," he said. "Call me when you're five minutes away and I'll meet you out front. You won't have to go in by yourself."

Her eyes brightened with gratitude. "That would be great. Plus, if the nerves get to be too much and I start vomiting uncontrollably, you can probably prescribe something, right?"

He laughed. "If necessary."

"Okay. Thanks, Josh. You've been great."

They stared at each other for a second, then she turned and walked away. He stayed where he was, watching her move through the diner, appreciating the sway of her hips and the swinging movement of her sleek hair.

Being alive suddenly didn't feel so bad.

"Did you like her?" Abbey asked the second Josh walked into the house. "I've always liked her. I think she's great, but what did you think?"

Josh bent down and kissed his sister-in-law on the cheek. "I liked her."

"Really?"

"I swear."

"Good." Abbey beamed at Pete. "He liked her."

"I heard."

Abbey had loosely pinned up her long, blond hair. The free ends bounced as she spun and hurried into the kitchen, waving for him to follow her.

"A couple of my friends are being protective about Crissy wanting to meet Brandon. They're afraid she's going to make trouble." Abbey opened the oven, then pulled out two freshly baked loaves of bread.

His mouth watered. Abbey had a lot of great qualities, and he'd always put her baking near the top of the list.

"She's looking for a connection," he said.

"That's what I said. All these years we've invited her to be a part of the family, but she's always held back." Abbey set the pans on cooling racks, then turned to him. "She has family, but they don't live around here. I've always wondered if she's lonely."

Pete sighed, then put his arm around his wife's shoulders. "Stop rescuing the world. Crissy is a very successful businesswoman. She doesn't need you messing in her life."

"I'm not messing. I don't mess. I'm just saying, she needs us."

Pete looked at Josh, then rolled his eyes. "Let it go," he said, with exaggerated patience. "Crissy's fine."

"Maybe we could fix her up with someone."

"She can get her own guy. Don't you have enough to worry about?"

Josh walked over to the cookie jar on the counter and reached inside. Abbey had made chocolate chip cookies the previous day and the four he'd eaten then hadn't been close to enough. Now as his brother and sister-in-law continued on with a very familiar argument, he munched on two more.

Pete and Abbey were the kind of couple who had been born for each other. From the first moment they'd met, they'd both known they would be together forever. There hadn't been any games or questions or even a discussion. They'd started dating their sophomore year of high school and from that first night, had known what their future would be.

"So she's coming to the party?" Abbey asked anxiously.

"That's what she said," Josh told her. "She wants to meet Brandon."

Abbey smiled. "That's good. We're all going to be one big family. She'll get to know him and relax and then he can know his birth mother." She turned to Pete. "What about Zeke? He's single."

Pete groaned, then glanced at his brother. "Escape while you still can. When she gets like this, she's impossible to stop."

Crissy was generally a fan of the whole weekend concept, but this time, Saturday had come along way too quickly. She'd spent the morning trying to figure out the right thing to wear to a "Hey, we're adopting" party. She wanted to make a good impression, but not stand out. Casual, but not too casual. Pretty, but not sexy.

She tried telling herself that Brandon was a twelve-year-old boy. He wouldn't even notice her. But still, every time she thought about meeting him there were jumping frogs where her stomach should have been.

She finally settled on a pair of tailored jeans, a lightweight fitted sweater and a leather jacket. Boots gave her some height. She fussed with her hair, did her makeup twice and generally spent more time sweating her appearance than she had on any first date in recent memory.

Not that she went on many first dates anymore. She hated them. Dating was miserable enough without dealing with the whole "get to know" first date.

After changing her earrings again, she walked out to the living room where her cat, King Edward, lay in a patch of sun.

"How do I look?" she asked as she turned in a slow circle. "If you were a twelve-year-old boy, would I embarrass you or not?"

King Edward raised his head, blinked twice, then yawned.

"Yeah, that's what I thought," she muttered, grabbed her keys and headed out.

In less time than it should have taken, she pulled up in front of a sprawling ranch-style house in a comfy suburban section of Riverside. It was the kind of street where kids rode bikes and neighbors took in packages for each other.

Crissy had to park a nearly half a block away, due to the number of cars. Josh hadn't been kidding when he'd said it was a big party. All the easier for her to get lost in the crowd, she thought as she climbed out.

She'd taken him up on his offer and phoned when she'd been on her way. As she approached, she saw him step out onto the small porch and head toward her.

He was taller than she remembered and oddly enough, better looking. She liked the way he smiled at her and tried to focus on him rather than her reason for being there.

"Nervous?" he asked as she approached.

"Paralyzed. I may start drooling."

"That will make an impression."

They stared at each other. He shoved his hands into his jeans pockets and smiled.

"It's okay. Take a breath. You'll do fine."

"Something you don't actually know," she muttered. "I have a fabulous imagination and I can come up with about three hundred disaster scenarios in less than a minute."

"Impressive."

He looked far too amused for her taste. "You could be more sympathetic here. It's my life on the line."

"It's not your life. It's nothing more than—"

But before he could attempt to convince her of the impossible, the front door banged open and a twelve-year-old boy burst onto the porch.

"Uncle Josh, come on! We're going to play football and I want you on my team."

Crissy's breath caught in her throat. The world seemed to jog slightly to the left. She stared into a face she'd only ever seen in pictures. But this flesh and blood version couldn't begin to compare to those two-dimensional photos.

She'd seen him in person once before. Nearly thirteen years ago, on a Thursday morning when the nurse had offered her the tiny, wrapped baby to hold.

Crissy remembered she'd refused. She'd pointed to a tearful but elated Abbey.

"That's his mom," she'd said, and meant it.

But did she still?

Chapter Two

Crissy tried not to stare at Brandon. This was their first meeting and she didn't want to come off as scary or creepy. But it was hard to act normal when her heart pounded so hard in her chest she was sure even the neighbors could hear it. Fortunately Brandon was far more interested in his game than an adult visitor he didn't know.

"I'll be there in a few minutes," Josh said. "Go ahead and start without me."

"Not if I want my team to win," Brandon said.

"Winning isn't everything."

"You always say that, but when we play you get mad if we lose."

Josh chuckled. "It's a character flaw. I want better for you."

Brandon rolled his eyes, but he was grinning.

"Uncle Josh, you know you want to play. I'll let you be quarterback."

"Bribery, huh?"

Crissy stood silent through their conversation. She tried to focus on Josh, but her gaze kept slipping to the tall, skinny boy pleading for victory. Looking at him was surreal—she could see parts of herself and her family in him. A familiar tilt of the head, a similar smile. She'd never thought about finding bits of herself in Brandon.

She was both delighted by the fact and a little disconcerted. The need to run was just as strong as her desire to know more about him. Talk about a series of complications.

Josh stepped close and put his arm around her. As the steady weight settled on her shoulders, she realized she'd been shaking.

"This is Crissy," he said. "She's a friend of mine. Crissy, this is Brandon Daniels."

"Hi," she said, doing her best to smile normally. "Nice to meet you."

"You, too," Brandon said automatically as his gaze shot back to his uncle. "You brought a girl?"

"It happens."

"It hasn't ever." Brandon was obviously intrigued by the idea. "So she's like your girlfriend?"

Josh didn't bring women around? Crissy knew he was close to his family, so did the lack of women mean he didn't date? He was single—she was sure Abbey had told her that. So why the lack of female companionship? On the surface he was practically perfect—good-looking, funny, charming and hey, a doctor. What was there not to like?

"She's female and a friend," Josh said easily. "Deal with it."

Brandon eyed Crissy, then grinned. "Okay." He moved close and held out his hand. "Nice to meet you."

Crissy shook hands with her son. A thousand emotions flooded her as their skin touched. This boy had been conceived inside of her, had grown in her body. She'd given birth to him and then walked away. They were strangers and yet as intimately connected as two people could be.

Too much, too soon, she thought as her head began to spin.

She turned to Josh. "You should go play. I'll be fine."

"All right!" Brandon rushed to the front door. "You heard her. Come on!"

"You sure?" Josh asked as he stepped back. "I don't want to leave you alone."

"She's fine," Brandon said. "She can find her way to the kitchen where my mom is." He backed into the house yelling, "It's the first door on the left." There was the sound of running feet followed by a faint, "I got Uncle Josh on my team."

Josh ushered Crissy into the house. They stepped into a messy but comfortable-looking living room.

"If you're sure," he began.

"Go." She pushed him toward the hallway. "Like Brandon said, I can find my way to the kitchen."

"Okay. But I'll be back soon."

He headed down the hallway. Before following and

finding the kitchen, Crissy looked at the pictures on the living room walls. There were dozens, all family photos. Baby pictures of Brandon gave way to snapshots of him at four or five with another baby. The infant grew to a pretty little girl. Then a third child joined the mix.

There were formal portraits and candid shots. Some with Abbey and Pete, some without. But wherever Crissy looked, she saw a connection. Did she have a right to step in the middle of this? Despite Abbey's constant urgings to get to know Brandon, Crissy felt like an outsider who had the ability to destroy this happy family.

"Something I won't do," she whispered to herself, making a vow rather than a statement. She was here to get to know her son, but not at the cost of hurting something wonderful. If anything bad started to happen, she would disappear and never be heard from again.

She walked down the hall and found her way into a large, bright kitchen. There were half a dozen women standing around, talking and laughing.

They looked like the clients who came to her gyms. Suburban moms. Normal women with busy lives. Once again Crissy had the sense of them being a part of something and not being sure if she would ever belong. Then Abbey looked up from the cutting board where she'd been slicing strawberries and saw her.

"You made it," she said, her voice bright with pleasure. "Everyone, this is Crissy. She's a friend of Josh's. Crissy, these are my friends. I'm going to go around the room and tell you everyone's name, but we don't expect you to remember them the first time out."

"Oh, yes, we do," a pretty redhead said with a laugh. "We'll quiz you later. Failing will mean dire consequences."

"Don't frighten her the first day," a blonde said. "Save that for her second visit. It builds anticipation."

"Ignore them," Abbey told her. "They're actually very nice."

Crissy sensed that. She tried to put names with faces, but got hopelessly lost. Part of the problem were the comments about her and Josh.

"I always knew that man was too fabulous to stay single long," one of the women murmured, almost regretfully. "Someone had to catch him eventually."

A by-product of the cover story, Crissy thought. By being Josh's friend, people assumed they were dating. Not that she would mind going out with him sometime. Just not now—when there was so much other stuff going on. Still, she accepted the teasing and continued meeting Abbey's friends.

When everyone had been introduced, Crissy was offered a choice of beverages, including white wine. She chose iced tea.

"Is the game starting?" Abbey asked, looking out the large bay window with a built-in cushioned bench. "Oh, my. Maybe some supervision is in order."

Several of the women nodded. "Remember last time when Aaron sprained his ankle?" one of them asked. "I swear, the man still thinks he's seventeen."

Abbey's friends drifted toward the back door, then out into the yard. When it was just the two of them, Abbey smiled at her. "I sort of asked everyone to leave us alone for a little while. So you could get comfortable. I hope that's okay."

"It's fine. This is a lot to take in." Crissy drew in a breath and tried to focus. "You're being really nice about all this. You could have refused to let me see Brandon."

"Why?" Abbey asked, looking genuinely confused. "The more family, the better. It's important for Brandon to know about his biological family. I'm thrilled you want to be here."

If their situations were reversed, Crissy wasn't so sure she would be as welcoming. "You're an amazing woman."

"Oh, please. I just want what's best for Brandon. I think your plan to take it slow is a good one for everyone." She continued slicing strawberries and then dumped them in a bowl. "I got in touch with Marty."

It took Crissy a second to connect the name with the football player she'd dated in high school. The one who had been her first time and Brandon's biological father.

"What did he say?" she asked, wondering if he was interested in Brandon as well. That would be fifteen kinds of weird.

"He's a lawyer in Boston. He was very polite, but told me that part of his life was finished. He'd signed away all rights to his child so if I thought I could get money out of him, I was sorely mistaken."

Crissy winced. "That can't have been fun."

Abbey shrugged. "Some people are like that— thinking everything is about money. He's moved on. I'm okay with that."

"He didn't have such a big stick up his butt when we

were dating in high school," Crissy said. "At least I don't remember seeing it."

Abbey grinned. "I'm sure you would have noticed."

Just then a pretty girl Crissy recognized from the pictures in the living room raced into the kitchen. "Hi, Mom. Can I have juice?"

"Sure." Abbey crossed to the refrigerator. "Emma, this is Crissy. She's a friend of Uncle Josh's."

The girl was about eight or nine, tall and skinny, with cartoon princesses on her athletic shoes.

"Hi," Emma said shyly. "Uncle Josh is really nice."

"Yes, he is," Crissy said, appreciating how easy he'd made things for her.

Abbey handed her a juice drink and the girl skipped toward the back door.

"You have your hands full," Crissy said. "I can't imagine raising three kids."

"I started with one, so that helped." She began pulling bowls of salads out of the refrigerator. "We've been lucky. All the kids have been great. Hope, the little one, just turned two, but she's still a sweetie. Right now she's down for a nap, but when she gets up you'll see what I mean. She's a real people person. Brandon is more athletic. A typical boy. Emma is the quiet one. Her idea of a good time is an afternoon spent reading. I love how different they all are, how their personalities grow with them."

The counter filled up quickly, so Crissy stepped in and took two large bowls from Abbey. She glanced at the contents.

"Did you make all this?"

Abbey shrugged. "Yes. I'm a bit obsessive about what my family eats. I go for organic and healthy whenever I can, which means I do a lot of cooking. We have a big garden on the side of the house. Brandon and Emma both help me with it. I make our bread and things like cookies and cakes. I'm a real homebody." She glanced at Crissy. "That probably sounds really boring to a successful businesswoman like you."

"Not at all," Crissy told her, trying to remember if she'd ever turned on the oven in her kitchen. "I'm not the least bit domestic. I wouldn't know where to begin. I've never baked anything. I can't even knit and I've been taking classes for months."

"But you're good at other things," Abbey said. "The whole work world. I think about getting a job sometimes. Money is tight, with us just living on Pete's paycheck. It gets worse when we adopt."

Crissy frowned. "I don't understand. If you've had Hope for the past two years, why would she cost more when you adopt her?"

"The state pays us to be foster parents. When we adopt, that money goes away." Abbey wrinkled her nose. "Some of my friends tell me to just keep them as foster kids. They'll still be ours. But Pete and I want to be sure the babies know they belong to us forever and that no one can ever take them away. When you're all alone, like Hope and Emma were, that's important."

"I had no idea," Crissy murmured. The only things she knew about the foster care and adoption system were what she'd seen on television or the movies. Not many people would be willing to give up steady income the way Abbey and Pete had, just to make a child feel secure. Especially when money was tight.

They lived in a different world, she thought, wondering if she would be willing to make the same kind of sacrifices. She'd always thought of herself as a basically good person, but when faced with Abbey's generous heart, she wasn't as sure about her character.

She glanced out the window and saw the football game in midplay. Brandon ran downfield and Josh tossed him the ball. Brandon leaped up into the air and gracefully caught the spinning ball, landed and dashed for the touchdown. As he crossed the goal line—marked by two lounge chairs—he grinned and did a little dance.

Crissy felt herself smile as she watched the boy. He was so happy and together. She liked his easy confidence and the way he threw himself into the game. She'd been that way about sports, too. In her world, there hadn't been room for second place. There was either a win or disappointment.

"He's very special," Abbey said, coming up to stand next to her. "In so many ways. You gave us a great gift when you allowed us to raise him."

Crissy felt overwhelmed by emotion. "I'm not here to make trouble. I swear."

"I know," Abbey told her. "You can stop worrying about that. I trust you to do the right thing for Brandon. You love him."

Love her son? Crissy had barely been willing to admit he existed. That wasn't love. Abbey gave her way too much credit. She didn't deserve this family's kindness.

"We'll take it slow," Abbey continued. "If things go well, you can tell him who you are."

"I won't do that without talking to you first."

"I appreciate that. Don't worry. Things have a way of working themselves out."

"You're too trusting," Crissy said. "The world isn't always a nice place."

"I'm wrong from time to time, but not often. Pete teases me that God looks out for the very young and the very naive. But he loves me anyway. Family is everything for us. We knew from the start we were going to have to adopt. Brandon was our first blessing."

"You have three blessings now. How many more are there going to be?"

Abbey's expression turned impish. "I'm hoping for seven, but don't tell Pete. He always clutches his chest and moans when I hint at four more."

Seven children? *Seven?* On *purpose?*

"I'm with Pete," Crissy murmured, unable to imagine what life would be like. Chaos, for sure.

"We'll see," Abbey said. "If we're done adding to our family, I'm happy. But if there are a few more kids who need a good home, then we'll make room. We've been lucky. It's been harder for Josh."

There was an opening Crissy couldn't ignore. "In what way?"

"You know he's a widower, right?"

Crissy shook her head, shocked at the news. "No. I didn't know. She must have died very young."

"Too young. Stacey was barely twenty-seven. Cancer. She'd had it as a child and it went into remission.

But she always knew there was a good chance it would come back and it did. She died very quickly, four years ago. Josh was devastated. For a while we wondered if he would make it. But he's finally getting better. Smiling more. Enjoying life. Dating."

Crissy tried to take it all in. Josh and Stacey couldn't have had very long together. She'd never lost anyone close to her and couldn't imagine how much that would hurt. Talking to him she wouldn't have guessed he'd been through so much. He was the kind of man who—

She caught Abbey looking at her, a knowing gleam in her eyes. Crissy replayed the conversation. One word stood out. Dating.

"Did you mean me?" she asked and took a step back. "Josh and I aren't dating. He's helping me with the whole Brandon thing."

"He's smiling," Abbey told her. "So are you seeing anyone?"

Crissy laughed. "You're trying to set me up?"

"Why not?"

"Complications. Josh is the last guy I'd want to get involved with." Their family connection—Brandon—made the situation impossible.

"He's a great guy," Abbey said.

"I already guessed that, but no thanks."

"Don't you think he's sexy?"

Involuntarily Crissy felt her attention being pulled to Josh as he ran across the backyard. His body moved with an easy grace and somewhere inside of her body parts sighed in appreciation. "He's okay."

"Nothing more?"

"No," she lied.

"Then I'll have to find you someone else."

Great. A matchmaker. "And if I told you I wasn't interested in romance right now?"

Abbey grinned. "I wouldn't believe you."

After dinner, Crissy collected plates and headed for the kitchen. Abbey called out to stop her.

"Crissy, while you're in the kitchen, would you grab the ice cream for the cupcakes? There are cookie sheets in the freezer with individual scoops in little cups."

Of course there were, Crissy thought, guessing Abbey took care of every detail.

"No problem," she said.

"Great. Brandon, honey, would you help Crissy?"

"Sure, Mom."

Crissy stumbled slightly, caught herself and continued into the house. Apparently Abbey's need to meddle didn't stop at romance. It seeped into every corner of life.

Crissy did her best not to panic. In truth, she'd totally avoided having any contact with the boy. She'd watched him play football before dinner and had listened to him chat with his parents' friends during the meal. She'd been observing rather than participating, wanting to get to know him without him being aware of her.

Now she walked into the kitchen, put the dishes on the table and wondered what she should say. The simple act of starting a conversation seemed impossible. Her brain went blank and her tongue stuck to the roof of her mouth.

Okay, she thought frantically. If talking wasn't going

to happen then she should act. She walked to the refrigerator and opened the freezer door. Then frowned.

"There's no ice cream."

"It's in here," Brandon said and led the way into a
large laundry room that held an upright freezer.

He opened the door and she saw cookie sheets covered with cupcake liners, each filled with a perfect
scoop of ice cream.

"Oh, my," Crissy breathed. "Your mom is so together
it's almost scary."

Brandon chuckled. "She's into feeding people. She's
always bringing cakes and cookies and stuff to school."

"That must make you popular."

"It helps." He pulled out one of the trays and handed
it to her, then took the second one himself.

"I don't cook much," she admitted. "My idea of a
home-cooked meal is to stop for a salad on the way
home."

Brandon wrinkled his nose. "Girl food," he muttered.

What? Girl food? "Hey, you don't get to think less
of me because I'm a girl. I saw you running during the
game and I could take you."

He snorted. "Yeah, right."

She might not know how to talk to a twelve-year-old
boy, but she knew exactly how fast she was when she
wanted to be.

"Want to put your attitude to the test?"

He glanced at her boots. "You gonna wear those?"

"Uh-huh."

"I don't think so. I'm fast."

"I'm faster."

Brandon stopped on the porch and looked at her. "If you think you're so tough, you can play in the next game. It starts right after dessert."

"You're on."

His eyes widened. "For real?"

"Yes, and when you see how good I am, you'll bow down and apologize."

He grinned. "*That's* not gonna happen."

Crissy shook her head. "You are so wrong."

The sun was close to setting, but there were plenty of lights on in Pete's backyard. Josh collected a beer from a cooler and walked over to one of the lounge chairs by the football game that was just starting. Despite Brandon's pleading, he'd refused another round. His nephew's enthusiastic tackle earlier than afternoon had left him bruised and limping.

As he settled down, he saw an unexpected addition to the lineup. His gaze narrowed in on a perfect backside sticking out during the huddle. Crissy? Playing football? He looked down at the ground. In those boots?

It didn't seem possible, but when they clapped and broke, she headed for the front line. Pete was across from her. She grinned.

"You're not going to stop me," she told him.

"That's what you think."

Crissy laughed, then turned and watched as the ball was snapped. Seconds later, she was flying down the field.

Pete and Abbey had bought the rambling old house because it had plenty of bedrooms for all the kids they wanted and because the yard was massive. They'd been determined to have the place all the kids in the neighborhood wanted to play. So there was plenty of room for Crissy to sprint downfield.

Despite what had to be three-inch heels on her boots, she moved with a speed that stunned the hell out of him. Brandon, normally the fastest guy on the field, couldn't keep up.

She suddenly stopped, turned and caught the ball, then raced between the goal line markers. She spiked the ball, then crossed to Brandon.

"You were saying?" she asked.

"You're totally bad," the boy breathed. "That was awesome. Even if you're a girl."

"So maybe now you'll stop underestimating what girls can do."

"I guess."

He looked stunned. Josh had to admit he was right there with him. He'd known that Crissy owned a couple of gyms and it made sense that she worked out, but he'd never guessed she could play like this. What would she be able to do in athletic shoes?

He told himself he could never go jogging with her. She would leave him gasping in the dust.

The two teams lined up again. This time Pete's team had the ball. They used a running play. Crissy was right there with Pete as he raced up field with the ball.

She was soon level with him, then she calmly reached over and plucked the ball from his grasp. He was so shocked by her action that he actually let go. Seconds later, she was running back the way she'd come. It was over in an instant. She crossed the goal line again.

Brandon yelled and ran over. They high-fived each other.

"Girls rule," she said.

"I guess," Brandon muttered.

Abbey settled in the seat next to Josh's. "I feel vindicated," she said. "We need more Crissys in the world."

"I'm thinking one is all we can handle."

"You know she'd kick your butt out there."

"I do, but you don't have to be so happy about it."

"Female solidarity." She leaned back in the chair. "It's going well."

He nodded. "Maybe it's going to work out. You all deserve that."

"Does the 'you all' include Crissy?"

"I'm not sure."

"You need to trust her. Pete and I do."

She and Pete had always been dreamers, believing the best in everyone. Josh had offered to act as go-between in this situation mostly to get to know Crissy so he could step in and prevent any trouble. Someone had to watch out for his brother and sister-in-law. But so far, he liked what he saw. Crissy hadn't tried to push her way into anything. She'd held back and observed. Maybe things would work out.

"She's not married," Abbey said.

He groaned. "Get off of me."

"Why? She's lovely. You can't tell me you can look at her and not notice that? She's so physical and smart. It's an irresistible combination."

He grunted because what was there to say? Yes, he'd noticed Crissy. She was all his sister-in-law said, plus sexy enough to make even *his* dormant body notice. But noticing was a long way from acting.

"You can't live like a monk forever."

"I won't," he said, even though he had no plans to change his current status.

"She's right there. Ripe for the taking."

He turned to Abbey and raised his eyebrows. "Are you serious? Ripe for the taking? Who talks like that?"

"I do. You need a woman."

This was a conversation he did *not* want to be having. "So you're suggesting I use Brandon's birth mother for sex?"

"You have to start somewhere and she's family."

"All the more reason to avoid her. Sleeping with Crissy isn't a complication any of us need."

"Fine. Sleep with someone else, I don't care. But you have to do something. Have you even been with anyone since Stacey died?"

There was no point in answering the question—they both knew the truth.

Josh didn't know how to explain that he wasn't interested in being with anyone. He hadn't been avoiding intimacy—he hadn't been tempted enough to bother. He had a feeling that part of him had died with his wife.

"I'm not asking you to risk your heart," Abbey said. "Just give the equipment a test drive. You might like it. You used to like it."

"I will not discuss my sex life with you."

"You don't have a sex life, or any life. That's my point." She turned to face him. "Josh, please. It's been long enough. You can't stay emotionally buried forever."

But that's exactly what he wanted. A life without emotion, without feeling. Because falling in love and then losing Stacey had nearly killed him. He wasn't willing to risk that again. Not for anyone.

Chapter Three

Crissy made it a point to leave with the first rush of guests. She didn't want to linger and create a potentially awkward situation. So far the visit had been easy and fun, which was a definite plus. Why mess with that?

She collected her jacket and her purse, then found Abbey in the kitchen. "Do you go into the other rooms of the house?" Crissy asked, her voice teasing. "Or is it just this one?"

"Only the kitchen," Abbey told her with a smile. "I sleep in the broom closet."

Pete strolled into the room. "Are you leaving? Thanks for coming. Things went well."

"I agree. You've both been great."

"We're happy to have you hang around," Abbey said. "What do you want the next step to be?"

Crissy didn't have a clue. "Can I get back to you on that?" she asked.

"Sure. Call me and we'll talk."

Crissy nodded and headed for the front door. She paused when someone touched her arm.

"Leaving?" Josh asked.

"Yes. But I wanted to thank you for all your help."

"Come on. I'll walk you out."

They moved into the night and headed for her car.

"Nice wheels," he said, nodding at her BMW 330i.

"An indulgence," she admitted. "I paid off two of my business bank loans and celebrated with some serious shopping."

"A car, not shoes?"

"I'm not your typical female."

"So I noticed. You play football."

She laughed. "I can hold my own. I'm fast. Tackling would be more of a problem. I lack the body mass to do any damage."

His gaze never left her face, but she had the oddest sense that he was checking her out. Which was crazy. Josh was acting as a mediator, nothing more. Besides, she wasn't looking to get involved with Brandon's uncle.

"Today went well," he said.

They stood in the dark, Crissy leaning against her car, Josh standing in front of her, his hands in his jeans pockets.

"It did." She'd been holding emotions at bay for hours and refused to give in to them now. "I was terrified, but it was okay. Brandon's amazing. Pete and Abbey have done a great job with him. With all the kids. They're an inspiration."

"Maybe they started with a good gene pool."

She shook her head. "I'm not taking any credit for that boy's personality. I don't deserve it."

"Still beating yourself up?"

"Regularly. I do it for exercise."

"You shouldn't."

"Easy to say," she told him. "Harder to do. I don't know what to think when I look at him. Is there connection? Should there be? Am I messing with his world? I'm so far out of my comfort zone, I don't know where to begin."

"You talked to him," Josh said. "How did it go?"

"Good. We talked sports mostly. I like him. I never thought about liking or not liking, but I do."

"Did you want to tell him who you were?"

If the car hadn't been right behind her, she would have taken a step back. "No. I don't know that I ever will. It's too soon. The situation is…complicated."

Whatever everyone else might say, she still wasn't sure she deserved to get to know Brandon. Adding to the mix was her desire to not hurt him or his family. The easiest thing would have been to stay away, but for some reason, she'd been unable to do that. Which left her an emotional mess.

Feelings welled up inside of her. She tried to ignore them, but when she had the unexpected and overwhelming urge to throw herself at Josh and ask him to make it all better, she knew it was time to leave. She didn't have breakdowns and if she was about to start, she would prefer they be in private.

"Thanks again," she said. "I appreciate your help."

"I was happy to be here. You have my number. Call me if you want to talk about any of this."

Exactly what Abbey had said, but somehow Josh's invitation was inherently more intriguing.

"Okay, I will," she said, even though she knew she wouldn't.

Crissy managed to park in her garage and made it all the way to her kitchen before the first tears fell.

"This is stupid," she said aloud. "I don't cry."

She hadn't in years. So why start now?

Logically she knew there were any number of reasons, the first of which was meeting Brandon. She glanced at the clock on the cable box, then added three hours. It was too late to phone her parents in Florida. Too bad, because she could have used hearing a friendly voice.

She pulled out the bottle of white wine she'd opened the night before and poured herself a glass, then left it on the counter and walked into the room she used as her home office.

Ignoring her computer and the comfy sofa she'd put on the opposite wall, she crossed to the closet in the corner and pulled open the door. Inside were her off-season clothes, several boxes of financial records and a shelf full of clear plastic containers. She pulled off the one that held all her odds and ends from high school and sat on the floor.

The top came off easily. Crissy began digging through prom pictures, yearbooks and hundreds of photos of her with friends. At the bottom, she found an old envelope containing only a few pictures. They were all of her while she was pregnant and there was a single photo of Brandon, right after he'd been born.

She spread the pictures out on the floor and gave in to the tears. She looked so young, she thought as she touched a photo of herself in a hideous pink maternity blouse. Young and scared, yet determined. Determined not to let the consequences of a single night ruin her life.

She knew that's what she couldn't forgive. That she'd never agonized over the decision. She'd simply decided to get rid of the "problem" as quickly and easily as possible. That meant finding a nice couple to adopt her baby.

She hadn't even tried to make it work. Hadn't considered upsetting her careful plans. What did that say about her? She'd given away her *child* and for twelve years, hadn't looked back.

Shouldn't she have been devastated? Shouldn't she have worried about him? Wondered? Missed him? There were—

Someone knocked on her front door. Crissy wiped her face and stood. As she walked into the hallway, she pulled the office door shut behind her. She wasn't expecting anyone and it seemed too late for kids selling candy for school.

She glanced out the peephole in the door and blinked when she saw Josh on her doorstep.

Great. After her meltdown she would look red and blotchy. There was no way to disguise the fact that she'd been crying.

She opened the door and tried to smile. "This is a surprise," she said. "Is everything all right?"

"That's my question," he told her. "I wanted to check on you. How are you doing?"

"Great."

"Liar. Can I come in?"

She stepped back to let him enter the house, then closed the door behind him.

"Can I get you something?" she asked. "I have an open bottle of wine."

"Sounds good."

She went into the kitchen and poured a second glass for Josh, then collected the one she'd ignored earlier and carried both back to the living room.

Josh stood by the fireplace. He took the glass of wine, then looked around. "Nice place."

"Thanks. It's kind of big for one person, but I like the high ceilings and the open floor plan." She pressed her lips together. Chances are Josh wasn't here to talk about her house.

She motioned to the sofa. "Have a seat."

When he was settled, she curled up in the corner and faced him. "I'm fine," she told him.

"That wouldn't be my professional opinion. Meeting Brandon is a big deal. It makes sense that you have a reaction to all that's going on."

"Is that what it is?" she murmured, then put her wine on the coffee table. "I feel guilty. That's the bottom line in all this. I feel stupid and unworthy. He's a great kid. I like him. But until recently, I never thought about him as a real person. I don't even know what I'm upset about. Am I mourning what I never had? But I never wanted it. I don't know if I want to be part of his world, or even if I should be. I don't know how to get over the fact that I was lazy."

"You were young. There's a difference."

"There might be a difference, but it's not an excuse."

He sipped his wine. "I remember when Abbey told me they were adopting Brandon. I was still in medical school, studying all the time. I went by their house the first day they brought him home. I'd never been around babies before—not without my mom to handle things. He was so small. Both Pete and I were terrified. It was the only time I questioned being a doctor."

That made her smile. "Because you couldn't handle one little baby?"

"Yeah." Humor brightened his dark green eyes. "But not Abbey. She was a natural. Loving, attentive and fearless. She could handle everything from cutting those tiny nails to treating a spiking fever. Pete learned because he had to, but for Abbey it was only joy. Sometimes I think she's doing what she was born to do."

"Abbey's a great mom," Crissy said, remembering the homemade everything and the ice cream scoops in the individual paper cups. "I agree it's her calling."

"So it was a cruel twist of fate that took away her ability to have children of her own. She'd only ever wanted to be a mom. You enabled that to happen."

Crissy knew in her head he was telling the truth, but in her heart, she didn't think she should get off so easily.

"Marty was my first serious boyfriend," she said. "Back in high school. He played football and was really popular. I had a lot of friends, too, even though I played sports. So uncool for a girl."

"I'll bet you did well."

"I did. I was fast and coordinated and I worked hard. I had a plan. Softball scholarship to pay for my college, then a high powered career in finance." She shrugged. "At least the scholarship part came true. I had a full ride. The day I got the letter I finally admitted to myself what I'd been avoiding for weeks. That I was pregnant."

She looked away, remembering that day. How she'd curled up on her bed and wished the baby away—something she'd done ever since she'd begun to suspect that having sex with Marty and not using protection had been a dumb idea.

"Marty was as shocked as I was," she told Josh. "We were each other's first time and stupid about birth control. He panicked, saying he didn't want a baby. Not for a long time. I didn't, either. I had a future and it didn't include being a single mom."

"You were only seventeen. That would have been a hard road."

"I talked to my parents and told them what had happened. They offered to do whatever they could to support me. I could live at home and go to community college. Mom would baby-sit while I was in class. They made it sound so reasonable."

"But you didn't want that."

She shook her head. "I wanted out. Marty signed the paperwork releasing him from responsibility as soon as he could and I started looking for a couple to adopt the baby."

"What's wrong with that?" he asked. "Why is that so horrible?"

"I don't know. It just is. I feel guilty about not feeling guilty enough."

"That has to sound crazy, even to you."

Despite everything, she smiled. "I'll admit it does. I just feel horrible about not caring enough. Not suffering enough."

"Because you would be a better person if you'd been emotionally crushed?"

"Maybe."

"You don't regret the decision, just your lack of remorse?"

Crissy hesitated. Did she regret giving up Brandon?

She searched her heart. "Pretty much," she admitted. "I'm not like Abbey."

"No one's asking you to be."

"But she's so great with the kids. She has all those domestic abilities. I don't. I have no natural female talents."

From where he was sitting, Josh thought she had a few. More than a few. But she wouldn't want to hear about him finding her sexy.

Her vulnerability drew him in, mostly because he sensed she was normally confident and in charge of her life. She was a successful businesswoman who had one weakness—her inability to forgive herself.

"We're not living in the 1800s," he told her. "Women don't have a single role. Everyone gets to make choices. You gave your baby to a couple who desperately wanted him. Where's the bad in that?"

"Oh, sure. Use logic. I'm talking about my irrational side here. I want to wallow in guilt and shame."

"What is there to be ashamed of? Having Abbey and Pete raise your son?"

Her gaze narrowed. "I'm not ashamed of that and Brandon isn't my son. He's theirs. They are possibly the most perfect parents I've ever met and as my parents did a hell of a job, I have fairly high standards. Who the hell do you think you are?"

Temper flashed in her eyes. Color stained her cheek and she was breathing hard. Damn, she looked good. He felt a stirring of pure lust. It had been so long that at first he couldn't figure out what the heat pouring through him meant. When he did, he nearly grinned. It felt good to be alive. How long had it been since he could say that?

"You think this is funny?" she demanded, rising to her feet.

"Not funny. Just interesting. Anger is more productive than self-pity."

She glared at him. "I can't believe it. Are you playing me?"

He put down his wine and stood. "A little. I had no idea there was such a drama queen hiding behind your power suit."

"Drama queen? I don't think so." She moved closer and pointed her index finger at him. "You're just so typically male. Whenever there's a situation that makes you uncomfortable or that you can't handle, you go for the easy putdown. The chick insults. Do you feel more like a man now?"

She breathed fury. He could see she wanted to hit him—or at least throw him out.

"Kind of," he said with a grin.

Then acting rather than thinking, he grabbed her upper arms, pulled her up against him and kissed her.

He felt her shock and half expected her to push him away. For a moment there was nothing but the warmth of her mouth on his and the heat flaring between them. He braced himself for rejection, but it never came. Instead she tilted her head slightly and kissed him back.

Nothing intimate, he thought, enjoying the softness of her lips as they brushed against his. She shrugged her arms free of his hold and put her hands on his shoulders.

He breathed in the scent of her body. The outdoors, the faint fruitiness of the wine and a feminine sweetness that was unique to her.

He rested the tips of his fingers on her waist and slowly moved to her back. She felt different than Stacey. Shorter, curvier. At the thought of his late wife, he prepared to drown in memories and guilt. But there was nothing inside of him but a growing hunger.

He shifted his hands higher, then slipped one up the back of her neck so he could bury his fingers in her short, silky hair. At the same time she erased the final step that separated them.

Her body pressed against his from shoulders to knees. His first impression was of heat and curves. Her breasts burned against his chest. Every cell of his body cried out for him to touch her. To feel the smooth, soft flesh, to taste her nipples and listen to her moan in pleasure. It had been four years since he'd been with a woman, but he remembered everything he wanted to do. It flashed into his mind, an X-rated movie starring the woman in his arms.

Knowing that wasn't going to happen, he focused on their kiss. He moved to her jaw and kissed his way to her earlobe. Once there, he drew in the bit of flesh and nibbled until she sighed and her grip on him tightened. Her skin was soft and hot and tempting in ways he'd never imagined. The sound of her breathing filled him with need.

He moved down her neck, going slowly, kissing his way to the open vee of her sweater. Only when he'd felt her heart pounding did he return his attention to her mouth.

She opened for him immediately. He slipped inside and when his tongue touched hers, he felt a jolt clear down to his groin. The wanting grew until it was an inescapable pulsing. He was hard and ready. He wanted her. He wanted to touch and taste every inch of her body. He wanted to make her writhe and scream and come, then he wanted to start at the beginning and do it again.

Crissy drew back slightly and stared at him. Passion darkened her eyes. "Wow," she whispered. "That was some kiss."

"I'm glad you liked it."

"'Liked' doesn't come close." She moved her hands down his arms, then dropped them to her sides. "I want to blame the wine, but I haven't had more than a sip."

"Me, either."

"So it's emotional intensity and chemistry?"

He didn't know what it was. The only thing he was clear on was that his body had come back to life and it felt damn good to be hard.

"It just is," he told her.

"Very profound for a guy who doesn't do touchy feely," she told him.

"I have untapped depths."

"I can tell."

He knew he should leave. She'd been through a lot today and probably needed some time to process everything.

He leaned in and kissed her cheek. "You going to be okay?"

"Sure. I'm a little shell-shocked, but I'll recover."

"You'll get used to being around Brandon," he said.

"I was actually talking about you."

That made him smile. "Yeah?"

"Oh, yeah. You had me close to screaming 'take me now, big guy.'"

She had his full attention. "How close?"

"You don't need to know that."

But he wanted to know. He wanted her to tell him that he wasn't the only one interested in the erotic next step.

She pressed her hand to his chest. "You are very unexpected, Josh Daniels. You're a good man and an amazing kisser. Seriously you should have a plaque or something."

He covered her hand with his, then drew her fingers up so that he could kiss them. He pressed his lips to the center of her palm and watched as her eyes dilated.

"I should go," he murmured against her flesh.

"Yes, you should."

She didn't sound exactly convinced.

"Or I could stay." He hadn't planned to say that, but as soon as he did, he knew that's what he wanted. To be with her. Alive for a single night.

She drew in a breath. "Staying would work, too."

It was all the invitation he needed. He drew her against him and pressed his lips to hers. She melted against him, rubbing her belly against his hardness. The friction felt good—right. He wanted more. He wanted to bury himself inside of her and explode, but that was for later. Right now he had a plan.

He slipped his tongue into her mouth, tasting her. She brushed against him, matching his intensity, circling him, driving him to the edge. He explored her back, then slipped his hands over the curve of her butt. He squeezed and she arched against him.

The movements of the age-old dance returned to him. Slowly he drew up the hem of her sweater, then pulled the garment over her head and tossed it on the coffee table. But instead of going right for her breasts— which was really what he wanted to do—he pressed his mouth against her now bare left wrist.

Using his tongue, his lips and his teeth, he teased, kissed and nibbled his way to the inside of her elbow. There he circled the sensitive spot until she gave a half-giggle, half-moan that made him smile. He repeated the action on her other arm.

When her breathing came in pants he asked, "Which way to the bedroom?"

She took his hand in hers and pulled him down a short hall and into the first door on the right. She touched a switch on the wall. A small lamp on a dressing table came on, illuminating the feminine space.

The room was done in various shades of pink. Light pink on the walls, a deep rose on the bed. It was the most girly space he'd ever seen and a contrast to Crissy's take-charge personality. He liked seeing this side of her.

"Are you afraid?" she asked as she turned to him. "There are pink ruffles and lots of lace."

"I can handle it."

She pulled his shirt out of his jeans and began unbuttoning it. "Yes, but can you handle me?"

"Let's find out."

He pushed her hands away, took her in his arms and kissed her. Now when he explored her back, he felt heated bare skin. Even though he skimmed across her bra strap, he ignored it for now. There would be plenty of time for that later.

He urged her backward until she reached the bed. When she was seated, he crouched in front of her and unzipped her boots.

"I can't believe you played football in these," he said as he tugged off the high-heeled footwear. "You could have broken a leg. Or worse."

She smiled. "You're such a guy. Women can do anything in heels. It's all a matter of practice and balance."

He took off her socks next and had to hold in a groan when he saw her painted toenails and a gold toe ring. How many more surprises were there going to be?

The throbbing in his groin increased every time he touched her. As he had her stand so he could unfasten her jeans, his arousal made a strong case for just going for it. He ignored the message and the way she looked in tiny bikini panties, tossed the jeans onto a chair, then drew her onto the bed.

He kicked off his athletic shoes before joining her. Then he stretched out next to her and stared into her eyes.

"You're so beautiful," he told her.

"The things men say to get lucky." She grinned. "But I choose to believe you."

"You should."

She was lovely. He let his gaze drift down her body. Her breasts were full and pale, threatening to spill out of her lacy bra. He could see toned muscle under smooth skin. There was a small gold hoop in her belly button that made his mouth go dry. Her legs were long and he had a sudden visceral image of himself between them.

He returned his attention to her face, then bent down and kissed her. At the same time he reached behind her to unfasten her bra. She put a hand on his chest.

"Hey," she whispered. "You're not naked. Naked is required."

"I have some important things I need to do."

"While I like the sound of that, fair is fair. You see mine, I see yours."

He chuckled. "I like how you think."

He stood up and took care of his clothes in a matter of seconds. When he moved next to her, she stroked his chest.

"Nice," she whispered.

He kissed her and again moved his hand behind her back to her bra. This time she turned slightly to help him. When the hooks were free, she tossed the bra off to the side.

Her breasts were perfect. Full and pretty, with tight

coral-colored nipples. He knelt between her legs and bent over so he could cup her breasts in his hands. He closed his eyes and savored the feel of her silky skin, then he brushed his thumbs against the tight tips.

His body did its damnedest to remind him that paradise was only a few inches away. Pressure in his groin increased, but he ignored it. As much as he wanted his own release, he wanted to please Crissy more.

He opened his eyes and watched as he touched her. He slid his hands down her ribs to her belly, where he circled the tiny gold hoop. She opened her eyes and smiled.

"My present to myself when I turned thirty a couple of months ago. A reminder to stay young."

"Do you really need it?" he asked, as he drew off her panties.

"Probably not."

He bent over and took her left nipple in his mouth. She tasted sweet. He sucked, then circled her, flicking her with his tongue. She groaned then put her hands on his back. The pressure of her fingers told him what she liked. He licked her skin, then blew on the damp spot. She shivered.

He moved back and forth, giving each breast thorough attention. When her legs stirred restlessly, he kissed his way down her belly.

He slid his hands up and down her thighs. As he nipped at the edge of her belly button, he circled his thumbs closer and closer to her center. At last he eased one thumb through her curls and felt her swollen wetness.

Instantly his arousal pulsed, but he continued to

ignore the need as he lowered himself onto the mattress, parted her flesh and pressed his tongue to her center.

She tasted sweet and salty and when she groaned, he nearly joined in. While he ached to be inside of her, he wanted to feel her body responding to his every touch. He wanted to learn what made her tremble and what made her scream. He wanted to be intimately connected, even just for a few minutes.

He explored her feminine center, then focused his attention on that one, most sensitive spot. He circled it, then brushed it with the flat of his tongue. He moved slowly at first, giving her a chance to anticipate the next move. Her hips pulsed in time with his actions, then moved a little faster as if urging him on.

He complied, then slipped a finger deep inside of her. He pressed up, finding her inner pleasure point, then rubbed it in time with his tongue.

She began to breathe faster and faster. Her hips moved and he felt her muscles tighten. There was a moment of stillness, then she lost herself in her orgasm.

Her body shuddered. He felt the waves of contractions tightening around his finger. He continued to caress her with his tongue, lightening his touch but keeping up the speed. It was only when she relaxed that he slowed and finally stopped.

He kissed the top of her thigh, then her belly. She opened her eyes and sighed.

"Score one for the home team," she whispered.

"I had fun," he said, almost surprised by the fact. But he'd enjoyed pleasing her. He'd enjoyed everything about making love with her.

His erection pointed out that he would enjoy life a lot more when it was his turn, but he ignored that.

"Fun does not describe what just happened," Crissy said with a smile. She reached for him. "Come here and I'll show you what I mean."

The second she touched him, he nearly lost it. He was shocked by the sudden pressure between his legs and it took every ounce of self-control not to give it up right there. Telling himself it had been a long time didn't make the situation any more comfortable.

Her touch was sure and erotic. Too erotic. He shifted closer and she guided him inside.

The soft, wet, welcoming heat of her body hardly made things better. He pushed in, filling her, feeling as if he could get lost in her forever.

He'd had big plans of impressing her with his endurance, but that plan turned to dust the second time he thrust in her. She felt too good. He wanted her too much. He pushed in again and again, feeling the pressure build. Then he gave himself up to it, increasing his specd, focusing only on the way she pulled him in and made him never want to leave. Another thrust, then another and he was lost.

Chapter Four

Josh woke early to light spilling into an unfamiliar bedroom. It took him a second to figure out where he was and remember what had happened the previous night. He lay on his side in Crissy's bed, his arm around her waist, his face close to her smooth shoulder.

Slowly, so as not to wake her, he rolled onto his back and stared up at the ceiling.

He'd made love with another woman. After he'd met Stacey, he'd known he would be content to be with her—and no one else—for the rest of his life. Yet last night he'd needed with a desperation that still stunned him. There'd been so much heat and wanting. How was that possible?

He braced himself for the flood of inevitable guilt, the sense that he had betrayed the woman of his dreams.

Somewhere in the house a grandfather clock ticked off the seconds, then chimed the half hour.

Nothing. Not a flicker of emotion, save the hunger to make love to Crissy again.

He closed his eyes. Now sadness joined the hunger as he recognized his lack of feelings for what they were—healing. In the four years since he'd lost Stacey, without even noticing it was happening, he'd managed to put his emotional psyche back together.

When she'd first died, he wouldn't have thought it was possible, but apparently the clichés about time healing wounds were true. He'd held on to the sadness, because it was all he had left. He loved Stacey—he would always love her—but he was no longer emotionally immobilized by her passing.

Which meant what? That it was time for him to start living again? Did he want that? Abbey had joked about him taking the equipment for a test drive. He'd done that and more. While he appreciated the fact that he'd moved on, a part of him would always be sad. Now Stacey was that much further away.

The bed shifted. He turned to his left and saw Crissy sitting up. She kept a sheet pulled up to her shoulders and her smile was a little tentative.

"Hi," she said, then sighed. "This is awkward. I think things will go easier if we just admit that we're practically family. You're Brandon's uncle and I'm his birth mother and if I start to hang around more, then you and I will see each other and that could be tense."

She paused to take a breath, then continued. "I don't do this sort of thing. Sleep with guys I barely know. It's never been my style. It was just a lot of things. The emotion of last night and the fact that you're incredibly sexy, which technically makes all this your fault. You should probably apologize."

He put his hands behind his head and gazed up at her. "You want me to apologize for being incredibly sexy?"

She nodded even as her mouth twitched. "Absolutely. It gives you an unfair advantage, which I'm sure you use on a regular basis. Now that I think about you, you owe me way more than an apology. What you did was just plain awful."

He held in a chuckle. "So *you* have no blame in this."

She widened her eyes. "None. I'm the injured party."

"I see. So the fact that I couldn't help myself because of how you taste and feel and sound means nothing."

Color stained her cheeks. "Not at all. You are solely responsible."

"Uh-huh. I can shift the blame to you in one sentence."

"Oh, please." She shook her head. "Not even a chance."

"Want to bet?"

"Sure."

"So what are the stakes?" he asked, keeping his voice deliberately low.

She looked innocent as she asked, "What would you like them to be?"

That got his body's attention. Heat raced south and he was ready for round two. Well, technically round three because they'd made love again in the middle of the night.

Then the sensible part of his brain pointed out that a little perspective wouldn't be a bad thing.

"Loser cooks breakfast," he said.

"I can't cook."

"Fine. Loser buys breakfast."

"Deal," she said. "So make it my fault. You have one sentence, big guy."

He reached out and covered her hand with his. "I haven't been with anyone since my wife died four years ago. I've been on a couple of dates in the past year, but they were disasters."

Emotions chased each other across her face. Josh watched as she started to speak, stopped, then just stared at him.

"I don't know what to say," she admitted.

"Aside from asking me where I want to have breakfast, there's nothing *to* say. I'm not trying to make you uncomfortable, Crissy. I want you to know that I don't do this sort of thing, either. We both got lost in the moment. Maybe that's not a bad thing."

"It's not," she whispered and squeezed his fingers. "Thank you for telling me. I'm not going to make a big deal out of anything, I'm just glad you can trust me. You can, you know."

"I know."

She was special. There was something about her that drew him in. He wanted to explore possibilities, something he never thought he would consider again.

She looked at him. "Really? Four years. That's a long time."

He shrugged. "I was never into empty sex. I like a

relationship to go with my intimacy. I got over volume about the time I graduated from college. I know—not the most macho thing to say."

"The best thing to say," she told him.

"It's the truth. I've had my work and my family. It's been enough."

She smiled. "You're saying sex is overrated?"

"Not after last night."

"I'm glad." She released his hand. "Okay, it's time to get serious. Because you're my guest, you can shower first. I'll go make coffee. Just let me use the bathroom for a second first. How does that sound?"

"Great." Especially considering there weren't any clothes close to the bed. Which meant she would be walking across the room naked. He couldn't wait for the show.

She dropped the sheet, exposing her full breasts, then turned gracefully and slowly moved to the closet. The view was only from the back but he appreciated every curve. His erection throbbed a couple of times as if reminding him that there was still fun to be had.

Josh ignored it and the need to touch her. For now it was enough to feel alive. It had been a very long time since he had.

Crissy poured coffee into two mugs. Josh walked in from his shower, barefoot, wearing jeans and his shirt, although the shirt was open. She had a tantalizing view of hard muscles and reddish-brown hair that arrowed down to his waistband as if leading the way to the promised land.

He was a typical guy, she thought as she sat across from him. He looked good in the morning. Too good. She'd washed off her makeup, brushed her teeth and tried to get her hair to look slightly less like a cat's barfed-up hairball. She'd only been mildly successful.

King Edward strolled into the kitchen. She bent down to pet him, grateful for the distraction.

She wasn't sure what to do with the information Josh had given her…about her being his first time since Stacey's death. She didn't want to make too big a deal of it, but she couldn't helping thinking it had to be significant in some way. He'd been right about one thing… that single sentence had changed her perspective.

"What are you thinking?" he asked.

"That you're a complication I wasn't looking for. If you were just some guy, this would be easier. But you're Brandon's uncle."

"You've already panicked about that."

"I'm not done with the initial panic. I'm torn. I kind of want to keep seeing you." Assuming he was interested, but she wasn't going to say that. She was a powerful woman and powerful women assumed they were wanted. "But if things don't go well, it's going to make the situation more difficult. So what makes the most sense is to just be friends. We can pretend last night never happened."

One of his eyebrows rose, but otherwise he didn't react. "If that's what you want," he said.

"It is." She spoke firmly. "Just friends with short-term memory loss."

"Okay. That's what we'll do." He sipped his coffee.

Crissy stared at him, trying not to act outraged.

That was it? She asked to be friends and he agreed? Shouldn't he protest or try to convince her? Hadn't she mattered at all?

He stood. "I should let you start your day."

What? "Sure. Fine."

She rose and tightened the tie on her robe, then led the way out of the kitchen. She told herself she should be relieved. Obviously Josh was a whole lot more shallow than she'd imagined. In fact he was practically a jerk. Good to know. Better to learn it now than later. She could simply pretend this had never happened.

She started down the hall toward the front door. Josh grabbed her arm and turned her toward him.

"Wait," he said, his eyes dark with passion. "About that friend thing. I'm not sure it's going to work."

"What? Why not?"

"I have a great memory."

Then he pulled her close and kissed her.

She was weak enough to go willingly. He felt good and sexy and when she leaned in close, she found out exactly what he had on his mind.

"So about this friend thing," he murmured against her mouth. "Are you really serious about that?"

She tugged off his shirt and let it fall to the ground. "Apparently not."

An hour later Crissy found herself right back in the same mess where she'd started. Naked and content, but not sure she'd done the right thing.

"Now what?" she asked as she rolled to face Josh, who looked like a very satisfied predatory male.

"Now you blame me for what just happened."

She waved her hand. "You're too sexy, all your fault, let's move on. This is going to be complicated."

"Yes, it is."

"Do you want that?" she asked.

"I don't not want it."

She played that one back in her mind. "Okay. So the friends-only thing?"

"Not likely."

Which left them where? They weren't dating. She didn't date. First dates were always disasters and she avoided them on general principle. Of course without a first date, it was tough to have a second or third.

"When it's over?" she asked. "You'll still have to see me. Won't that be uncomfortable?"

"I'm confident we can get through it."

She wasn't as sure. "I tend to walk away from my exes," she admitted.

"I don't have a lot of history in that department," he admitted. "Want to see if we can handle it either way?"

Crissy knew she would be a fool to do anything but agree. Josh was a warm, caring, sexy man who wasn't afraid of falling in love. His four years of celibacy more than proved his devotion. Plus, he was a doctor and that would make her parents very happy.

But were there dangers, too. Playing it by ear was fine while things were going well, but if they ended badly, would that hurt her potential relationship with Brandon? Pete and Abbey might not look kindly on an ex-girlfriend of a beloved family member.

There was also the matter of her heart. Josh was a

great guy. But even though he was pretty damned close to perfect, there could be one major flaw—he might still be in love with Stacey. Did she want to risk falling for someone who couldn't love her back? Was it light years too early to be having this mental conversation?

Josh sat up. "Okay, you're taking too long to answer the question. You really do want us to just be friends."

"It's not what I want," she admitted, "but I think it's the most sensible solution."

She couldn't tell what he was thinking. Did it matter? She'd long ago learned the only person who was going to take care of her was her.

He leaned in and kissed her. At the first brush of his lips, she desperately wanted to take it all back and jump back into bed with him. An action simplified by the fact that they were already in bed.

"It's your call," he said. "We can be just friends. But I refuse to forget what happened."

She was neatly torn in two. Part of her applauded her rational, mature decision. The other part snorted in disgust and warned her she would be very sorry to be sleeping alone tonight.

"I won't forget, either," she told him, and meant it.

Crissy arrived at her friend Noelle's house in the early afternoon. She was still tingling from the previous night—and morning—and trying to deal with all the waves of feeling rushing through her.

For the past couple of years, her life had been relatively calm. She worked hard, grew her business, hung out with friends and avoided romantic complications.

King Edward, her cat, was enough of a live-in companion. She didn't need a man.

But in the space of less than twenty-four hours, everything had changed. She'd met Brandon and had slept with Josh. Both events had the potential to put her life into a wild spin. Not that she regretted either.

She walked up to the front door, but before she could knock, Rachel opened it and grinned at her.

"Welcome, my nonpregnant friend, for an afternoon of hormones, swelling and talk about birth and other fluids," Rachel said with a laugh.

Crissy smiled at her. "You're trying to scare me off and I refuse to show fear. Besides, your pregnancy is only a rumor. So far I haven't seen any evidence of a baby."

Rachel turned sideways and pulled up her loose sweater. Underneath, her jeans were unbuttoned and there was a definite tummy showing.

"It's a rice grain," Crissy teased. "Congrats."

The two women hugged.

"I wouldn't mind a rice grain," Rachel said as she shut the door and started toward the family room. "It would be a whole lot easier to pop out than an actual baby."

"But finding clothes would be tough, and what about the diaper situation?"

"Good point."

Crissy walked into the family room of the elegant home and saw Noelle half sitting, half lying on the sofa. She was seriously pregnant, her belly swollen to the point of looking painful. But despite her awkward size, she looked beautiful and content.

"Renoir should be here to paint you," Crissy said as she crossed to her friend, bent down and hugged her. "You look radiant."

"I feel good," Noelle said as she patted her belly. Her blue eyes glowed with happiness. "We're nearly there."

Rachel carried out a tray with three glasses and a pitcher of iced tea that Crissy assumed was herbal. She sniffed the air and detected the scent of something yummy.

"You didn't make food, did you?" she asked Noelle. "In your condition?"

"I put frozen food on cookie trays and stuck them in the oven. Hardly hard labor."

"She's saving that for later," Rachel said, her green eyes bright with humor. "Get it? Hard labor."

"Sometimes you two make me feel old," Crissy muttered as she dropped her purse on the floor by the chair then walked into the kitchen to bring back the snacks.

She'd known Noelle and Rachel less than two years, but the three of them had become very close. They'd met in a knitting class, randomly choosing the same table. Despite their differences in age and circumstances, or maybe because of them, they'd become close friends.

Nearly nine months ago, Noelle, nineteen and the sheltered daughter of a minister, had given herself to her soldier boyfriend. That single night had left her pregnant. When he was killed in Iraq, she hadn't known what to do. But rescue had arrived in the form of the boyfriend's older brother. Devlin Hunter had proposed a temporary marriage of convenience to give the baby a name and Noelle a head start at motherhood. The practical arrangement had quickly turned into a love match.

A few months later Rachel, a conservative kindergarten teacher, had had a wildly unexpected night of passion with an undercover cop. It, too, had produced a pregnancy. Rachel had been more than prepared to be a single mother, but Carter Brockett had other plans. When his family had meddled, they'd pretended to be a couple to throw them off. But the game had turned real and now the two were happily engaged.

Crissy joked that the way her friends had gotten pregnant so easily, she was only going to drink bottled water just in case. Not that she'd had cause for concern. It wasn't as if sex had been a big part of her life. She hadn't been with a man in—

She picked up the platter of tiny quiches and mini quesadillas, only to set it back down. Her stomach flipped over, her chest tightened and she felt a distinct tingling in her hands.

She and Josh had made love three times and neither of them had thought to mention or even use protection.

She wasn't worried about her health. He'd been in a monogamous relationship for years and celibate since then. She knew she was okay, which was all good news. But what about getting pregnant?

"No," she said aloud. "It couldn't. Not so fast."

She glanced at the calendar on the wall and did a quick calculation. It was a little early for her to be in a dangerous time. She was fine. Pregnant? No way.

That decided, she picked up the tray and returned to the family room.

Rachel had taken a seat in one of the overstuffed chairs, leaving the sofa for Crissy and Noelle.

"Does it hurt?" Rachel asked, eyeing Noelle's stomach. "It has to hurt. I don't like pain."

"I feel a little overstuffed," Noelle admitted. "But in a good way. The baby's moving all the time now. It's awe-inspiring to know there's life inside of me. Of course, sometimes I'm terrified, too."

"Of being a mother?" Crissy asked.

Noelle nodded.

"Don't be," Crissy told her. "You're a natural. Have been from birth. You'll do great."

"I hope so," Noelle said. She looked at Crissy. "Do you remember much about your pregnancy? Or should I not ask you that?"

She'd told both her friends about her past and her plans to meet Brandon.

"Almost nothing," Crissy said. "I tried to block it out of my mind at the time. Then when I couldn't ignore the situation any longer, I just didn't think about it. I didn't show much. The doctor said it was because I was so young." She smiled at Noelle. "Although you're still a baby, too."

"I'm growing up fast."

"Speaking of your pregnancy," Rachel said. "Tell us everything."

Crissy stared at her. How had Rachel guessed there might be a problem? That she and Josh could have, maybe, possibly, done a little life creating of their own? Was there a flashing sign over her head?

"Brandon," Rachel added. "You were going to meet him yesterday? How did it go?"

Relief came quickly. Crissy shook off thoughts of

being pregnant. She wasn't. She would get her period and then she would give herself a stern talking-to on the subject of jumping to conclusions, not to mention the importance of birth control.

"It was good," she said. "Strange and scary, but good. He's a great kid. Funny and athletic. Basically a sweetie. I liked him."

"Is that a surprise?" Noelle asked.

"I don't know. There's the whole issue of who I thought he was in theory and who he is in real life."

"Do you want to get to know him more?" Rachel asked.

"I do. But slowly, and I'm not sure about telling him who I am. Does he really need that information?"

"Would you want to know your birth mom?" Rachel asked. "I would. Family is everything."

Crissy knew her friend's past made that statement true for her. But Brandon hadn't had to discover that the hard way. He'd been surrounded by love from the moment he'd been born.

"I don't question my decision to give him up," she said slowly. "But I don't want to mess up what he has. His parents are amazing. I like Abbey so much. She's a lot like you," she told Noelle.

"Then she's obviously a superior person," Noelle said with a smile. "I know you're worried about making a selfish decision, but this isn't one. Brandon can have both you and Abbey in his life. When it comes to being loved, more is better."

"I just don't want to mess up," Crissy said. "Abbey called this morning and invited me over to lunch one day. Just with her and the kids. Casual. I want to go but…"

"You should." Rachel grabbed a couple of the quiches. "You have to forgive yourself sometime."

"Technically I don't."

"Rachel's right," Noelle said gently. "It's the only way to get on with your life. You don't want to be stalled forever."

Okay, sometimes friends were a pain in the butt, Crissy thought, both appreciative of the caring and slightly uncomfortable with the turn in the conversation.

"Enough about me and my problems," she said. "What's new with you two?"

"My mom's giving me a baby shower," Noelle said. "I'd really like both of you to come."

"I'll be there," Rachel told her. "I love showers."

"Me, too," Crissy said. "The being there part. Showers aren't my thing, but my love for you is big enough to overlook that."

"I'm flattered," Noelle said, then shifted on the sofa. "And while we're on the topic, I was talking to Dev yesterday and there's this guy at his office. He runs engineering, which sounds nerdy, but I've met him and he's gorgeous. Funny and smart. And single."

Crissy held in a groan. "How is that on the topic?"

"It's not, but I didn't have a good transition."

"Thank you, but no. I'm not interested in being set up. I don't date. I especially don't first date. And a blind date is a whole new level of dating hell. I'm not going there."

"But if you don't start going out, you'll be alone forever." Noelle sucked in a breath. "I'm seriously pregnant. You have to do what I say."

"Not really."

Noelle looked at Rachel. "Help me."

"No way. Crissy is the most together person I know. If she wants to stay single, that's her business. Some women prefer not to be with a man. They're happy on their own."

Crissy had been pleased with the support, right up until that last statement. It made her sound like someone who was going to live a scary life of filling rooms with newspapers and cats. Which reminded her she hadn't taken the Sunday paper out to the recycling bin—and she did own a cat.

"I'm not abnormal," she muttered. "I like men. It's dating I object to."

"When was the last time you went out?" Noelle asked. "Was it even this year? Or last year?"

"Ask the more interesting question," Rachel teased. "When was the last time you had sex?"

The two women grinned. Crissy didn't know what to say. This time yesterday, the answer would have been depressing. This morning—not so much.

Rachel picked up her glass of iced tea, then put it down. She stared at Crissy. "Oh my God. What's going on? You have the weirdest look on your face."

Crissy touched her cheeks, not sure what she was doing. "Nothing. I'm fine."

Noelle stared at her. "You're not fine. You're blushing. She's blushing, right?" she asked Rachel.

Rachel leaned forward, peering. "You've had sex. Recently. You look smug and guilty."

"I do not. Nothing happened."

Rachel flopped back in the chair. "She's lying."

"I know. And to women in our condition." Noelle looked disapproving. "Who is he? Start at the beginning and tell us everything. I have nowhere else I have to be today. I can outwait you."

Crissy opened her mouth, then closed it. She knew if she told them she wasn't ready to talk about it, they would both back off. But some part of her wanted their take on the situation.

"It's Josh," she said. "Brandon's uncle. The one I met with first to talk about the whole me-getting-to-know-Brandon thing. He invited me to a party at Abbey and Pete's house to celebrate the adoption of their new baby. Josh was really sweet and I liked him."

"Apparently," Rachel said. "So when did you get naked?"

Crissy ignored her.

"He was really nice to me at the party. I did okay until it was time to leave. Then I felt all these emotions crashing in. I barely got out of there before I lost it."

Noelle reached out and touched her hand. "I'm sorry you had to go through all that."

"It's my own fault," Crissy said. "I'm the one who's been avoiding the fact that I have a son. Anyway, I got home and had a good cry and then Josh showed up. He wanted to know if I was okay. We talked and then he kissed me and well, things sort of went from there."

"How was it?" Rachel asked.

Crissy grinned. "Amazing. Fabulous. That earthquake you felt last night? That was us."

Noelle sighed. "The only bad part about being this

pregnant is that I miss making love with Dev." She covered her mouth with her fingers. "Oh. Did I say that out loud?"

Rachel laughed. "Yes, and I'm taping this conversation."

Noelle turned to Crissy. "So this is good, right? You like him, he likes you. All positive."

"I don't know. It's an unusual situation. I'm trying to get to know the child I gave up for adoption. Josh is his uncle. If we get involved and then it ends badly, it will be awkward and uncomfortable for everyone."

Noelle shook her head. "You aren't going to keep seeing him, are you?"

"I suggested that we just be friends," Crissy said. "It makes the most sense. Brandon is my priority. I want to get to know him. Being involved with Josh would only get in the way of that. Josh agrees."

Neither Noelle nor Crissy looked convinced.

"So you'll still see him, but only as friends?" Noelle asked.

"We're not going to date or anything, but I'm sure I'll run into him."

What she would never admit to either of them was how much she was looking forward to that.

"You like this plan?" Rachel asked.

"Yes. It's the right thing to do. For everyone."

"But you've been lovers," Rachel pointed out. "Taking a step back after that is difficult. I know. Carter and I tried it. And didn't make it work."

"This is a totally different situation," Crissy said. "I'm not pregnant with his baby."

Her stomach flipped over again, but she ignored the

sensation. She wasn't pregnant. She was fine. Totally and completely fine. She had to be.

"I can handle things," she insisted. "Josh is great and I'm happy to be friends with him. We get along. Romance isn't required to enjoy each other's company. I'm tough."

Noelle smiled ruefully. "I can't help thinking being tough isn't going to help you this time, Crissy."

Chapter Five

Crissy didn't think it was a big deal to *be* nervous for her lunch with Abbey and the kids as long as she didn't *act* nervous around them.

Casual, she reminded herself. Abbey had stressed that it was nothing more than a casual lunch. Brandon and Emma were home because it was teacher meeting day at school. They'd spent the morning playing with friends and Crissy was going to stop by and join them for lunch. No biggie, right?

Except she was both terrified and excited. It was a case of nerves plus.

Still, she forced herself to walk calmly to the front and ring the bell. She was braced and prepared. Or so she thought until Brandon opened the door and grinned at her.

"Hey, Crissy," he said. "I told my friends how good

you were at football and they didn't believe me." He sighed heavily. "I didn't bother telling them you were wearing those high heels. That would have made them laugh. They just don't think a girl can be good at football."

Her heart stuttered in her chest as she stared into a face that shared features with her own. This was her son. Her baby. Twelve plus years ago, she'd given birth to him. He was alive because of her body. The information was both amazing and hard to believe.

"You know the truth," she said with a smile. "Sometime I'll come play with you and we'll blow them away."

"Yeah. That'll show 'em. Come on. Mom made soup. It's really good and the hard part is it cooks forever. I've been telling her I'm hungry for days, but she says we have to wait until it's ready."

She followed him into the kitchen and found Abbey putting what looked like rolls into the oven. But not any kind of store-bought, cook-for-a-few-minutes rolls. These were freshly made or risen or kneaded or whatever it was people did to make bread.

She laughed, then smiled at Abbey. "I just realized I don't even know how to make bread. I'm totally useless in the kitchen."

"Bread is nothing. I can show you, if you'd like. The way you work out, kneading would be easy. My hands always get tired." She put the cookie sheet in the oven, closed the door, then straightened and walked over to give Crissy a hug. "How are you?"

As all three kids were in the room, Crissy only

smiled and said, "Good." No point in admitting her nerves in front of an audience.

"Emma, do you remember Crissy? She was here for Hope's party."

Emma, a pretty eight-year-old, looked up from her coloring book and smiled. "Uh-huh. She's Uncle Josh's girlfriend. When they get married can I be a flower girl?"

Brandon made a gagging sound, then slumped down at the kitchen table and picked up a handheld video game sitting there. "Uncle Josh isn't going to get married."

"How do you know?" Emma asked. "I could wear a princess dress."

"Yes, you could," Abbey said, giving Crissy an apologetic shrug. "But Uncle Josh and Crissy are just friends. So there isn't going to be a wedding." Her expression turned teasing. "At least not anytime soon. Although it would be very good for Uncle Josh to get married again."

Emma wrinkled her nose. "You're talking about Aunt Stacey. I don't remember her. Sometimes when I look at pictures of her, I can kinda remember, but not now."

"She was okay," Brandon said, never looking up from his game. "She didn't like boys as much as girls."

Crissy felt miles out of her league with this conversation. She wanted to bolt to the other room, put her hands over her ears and hum loudly until the subject changed. Right up until Brandon's last comment.

"That's not true," Abbey protested. "Aunt Stacey loved you very much."

Brandon shrugged. "Not really. She was nice and everything, but she always brought Emma ribbons for her hair and ruffly things. She never brought me anything."

A protective, maternal instinct Crissy hadn't even known existed welled up inside of her. How dare Stacey ignore Brandon. Sure, girls were easier to relate to when one was female and didn't have any children of one's own, but that was no excuse to ignore a wonderful boy like Brandon. Or any boy, for that matter.

"She was more comfortable around girls," Abbey admitted, "but that doesn't mean she didn't care. I'm sure if she knew you wanted ruffly things, she would have brought them for you."

Brandon looked up, his expression disgusted. "I don't want girl things. I'm a boy. B-O-Y. Try to remember that."

"Yes, of course."

Abbey waved at the kitchen. "So, Crissy, welcome to the madness. What can I get you to drink?"

"Whatever you have that's easy."

"How about a diet soda? They're my guilty pleasure. Some people drink or smoke, I long for diet soda."

"Sounds great."

"Juice!"

The imperious command came from the blond toddler in the playpen beside the table.

Abbey turned to the little girl. "Are you thirsty, Hope?"

"Juice!"

Without turning his attention from the game, Brandon reached out and ruffled her hair. The affectionate gesture impressed Crissy and tugged on her heart.

"I'll get it," Emma said as she put down her crayon.

While Abbey got two cans of diet soda out of the refrigerator, Emma collected a juice box. Crissy saw from the label that it was organic with no added sugar. Typical, she thought, comforted by Abbey's consistency.

Crissy settled on one of the bar stools by the island where she wasn't in the way and didn't crowd the kids. This *was* supposed to be a low-key lunch.

"Did Brandon tell you he was bragging about your sports ability?" Abbey asked as she collected an apple, some grapes and a bowl.

"He mentioned his friends didn't believe a girl could be good at football," Crissy said. "In high heels, no less." She turned to Brandon. "I've always played sports. In high school, my softball team won the state championship."

He actually put down his game and looked at her. "Wow. That's cool. What position?"

"Second base. I was one of the top three hitters, too."

"Why softball and not baseball?" he asked.

"Girls couldn't play baseball."

"That's stupid."

"It is." Abbey sliced the apple into sections. "Either gender should be allowed to play any sport they want."

"Yeah," Brandon said. "If they're good."

Not wanting to make too big a deal of Brandon, Crissy turned to Emma. "What do you like to study in school?"

The girl looked at her. "I like reading and math. I like it when we study animals."

"Emma's great at math," Abbey said proudly. "She's working two grades ahead, which is amazing. I was never good at math."

"I always liked it," Crissy said. "I majored in finance in college."

Abbey wrinkled her nose. "Athletic and good in math. Under other circumstances I'm not sure I could like you."

"So speaks the woman who grows and bakes and does everything perfectly."

"Not perfectly," Abbey said with a smile. "But close."

"Want to see the book I'm reading?" Emma asked.

"I would," Crissy told her. As Emma ran off, Crissy turned to Brandon. "Do you like to read?"

He glanced up from his game. "Sure, but don't tell the guys. It's not cool."

"Of course not."

Emma raced back with a book about a girl who discovers she's a princess.

"Looks like a great story," Crissy said. "I love princess stories."

"Me, too." Emma beamed.

Brandon rolled his eyes.

Abbey put the fruit on the table, then collected Hope and set her in a high chair.

"We read a lot in our family," she said. "Most evenings we read instead of watching TV. Pete and I read aloud to the kids. It's fun."

Brandon put down his game, then crossed to the kitchen sink and washed his hands. When that was done, he collected flatware and napkins.

"We go camping every summer," he said as he set the table. "The lake where we stay has good fishing. Dad and I go out on a boat and catch stuff. Then Mom cooks it."

Crissy's idea of fishing was to pick something off a menu. "So who cleans the fish? Don't you have to do stuff to it before you can eat it?"

Brandon gave her the smile of a big, macho guy dealing with a frightened little woman. "Dad and I do that. Mom doesn't want to know about fish guts."

Abbey shuddered. "You got that right."

"I don't fish," Emma said. "I don't want to hurt the fish."

"I'm with you," Crissy told her. "We used to camp when I was little, but there was no fishing."

"Where do you think the tuna comes from?" Brandon asked.

"Tuna trees." Crissy grinned. "It grows right in the can. The tuna orchards are huge. I think they're in Idaho somewhere."

"I've seen pictures." Abbey smiled. "Pete loves the outdoors. Both he and Josh head off for a guy weekend a couple of times a year. They come back looking very scruffy. One camping trip a year is enough for me."

"Next year I get to go with them," Brandon said proudly. "Just us guys."

"Very cool." Crissy sipped her diet cola. "When we went camping it was just Dad and the kids. My mom stayed home. She loved the time to be by herself and relax. She said it was good for my dad to realize how much work raising three kids should be." She looked at Abbey. "You could take a lesson from that."

"I don't know," Abbey began.

"She won't stay home," Brandon said, sounding both pleased and disgusted. "She and Dad can't be apart that long. They need each other. They're always kissing and stuff. It's gross."

Abbey blushed slightly. "It's true. We spend so many nights apart because Pete's at the fire station. When we got married, we vowed we wouldn't spend any other nights apart, and so far we haven't."

Wow—that was nearly as impressive as the freshly baked bread.

"I'm with you on the grossness of parental affection," Crissy told Brandon. "My parents are still all over each other. It creeps me out. But it also makes me feel good to know they're in love and want to be together. It makes me feel safe."

Brandon looked at her. "Yeah," he said slowly. "Me, too."

It was one of those perfect moments of connection. She felt he saw her as someone he could like. She felt the same about him. He was more than a good kid—he was a good person. Which made this a very good beginning.

Josh stood in front of the all-female gym and wondered if he would be allowed inside. Not that he was here to work out. He'd stopped by to see Crissy.

He'd been unable to stop thinking about her, which was unusual for him. Her claim that they were just friends had given him a reason for his visit. Friends were allowed to stop by and see where each other worked. She was welcome in his office whenever she wanted and he was going to assume he was welcome here. As long as he could get past the front door.

He opened one of the large glass doors and stepped

into an open and bright reception area. The space was open, with plenty of natural light. The twenty-something woman behind the curved desk raised her eyebrows.

"Are you picking up someone?" she asked. "I can page her."

"I'm here to see Crissy Phillips. I'm a friend."

The woman's expression turned knowing. "Right. Go on upstairs. Her office is the last one on the left. Tina, her assistant, can show you in."

He climbed the stairs to the second floor. Below he could see the gym itself, with the modern equipment, along with several exercise classrooms. Three of the four were filled with women working out. Interesting place.

He found Crissy's office and introduced himself to Tina who waved him in. Then he opened a large wooden door and stepped into a big office that looked more like an executive corner office than a room above a gym.

Crissy had done well, he thought as he took in the windows, the view, the built-ins and the woman herself wearing a headset and pacing between her desk and the bookshelves.

"I'm not reasonable," she said pleasantly. "It's not in my job description. What is in my job description is to enforce the contract we signed. I have a delivery date and I expect you to keep it." She paused. "Uh-huh. I *am* a ballbuster. You bet. Okay, George. See you next Tuesday."

Josh watched her move, enjoying the way his body responded to hers. He also realized that he'd missed being around her. Not just for sex but for conversation and company. What did that say about him? About them?

She turned and saw him. Her eyes brightened and she smiled with so much pleasure that he felt like a hero. Damn, how did she do that?

She hung up and pulled off the headset. "You're a surprise."

"I was on my way to the hospital," he said, crossing to her and kissing her cheek. "I had a little time so I thought I'd stop here and see what all the fuss is about."

"Fuss?" She raised her eyebrows. "You're calling my life's work a fuss?"

"What are you going to do about it?"

Her smile returned. "I work out. I could take you."

"I don't think so."

He liked that they were teasing, that she was still comfortable with him.

"Pretty confident, aren't you?" she asked.

"I am. I heard about your lunch with Brandon. Abbey said it went well."

"It did." Crissy motioned for him to take a seat on the brightly colored sofa in the corner. She settled across from him in a chair. "I was terrified, but things went great. He's a great kid. Funny and charming. I want to take credit, of course, but it's mostly Abbey and Pete."

"You get credit for Brandon being smart. Intelligence passes through the mother."

"Really?" She looked pleased. "Are you just saying that?"

"There have been scientific studies."

"Cool." She chuckled. "So all those rich guys who

married beautiful women who weren't the brightest bulbs are going to be disappointed, huh?"

"I doubt they read the study."

"But brainy women everywhere are celebrating. Brandon reminds me a little of my brother. The way he moves and teases. There's also some of his father in him, but that's to be expected. It's interesting to see the blend of families."

He leaned back against the sofa. "Assuming you tell him who you are, will your parents want to meet him?"

"They would love to." Her humor faded. "They were very supportive when I found out I was pregnant. I think on some level they wanted me to keep him. He's their first grandchild. Both my sister and brother have married and have kids, so there have been others, but they've never forgotten him."

She shrugged. "I can't complain. They never made me feel guilty. They wanted me to make the best decision."

"Which you did."

"Thanks for saying that. I go to the bad place and remind myself I made the *easy* decision and should be punished for the next hundred and fifty years."

"You're the only one talking about that."

"I know. I need a new theme. It's just that I have so much and I wonder if I deserve it."

He glanced around. "Looks to me like you worked your butt off for this. Anyone hand you the business?"

"What? Of course not. My parents helped a little with the initial funding on my first gym, but I paid them back an incredible rate of interest and since then, I've handled all the money myself. I've done well."

"So be proud of that and let the rest of it go."

She looked at him and he felt the intensity of her gaze all the way down to his gut.

"You do go for logic," she murmured. "I can't decide if that's a flaw or not." She stood. "Come on. I'll give you a tour of the place and then you can be even more impressed."

She was already fairly impressive. Smart, beautiful, successful. Great in bed.

Not that he was going to think about that now. He didn't want to have to worry about everyone knowing what was on his mind as he toured the gym.

She showed him the offices upstairs. This was her primary location, with all the other gyms being handled through this office.

"Obviously we won't tour the locker rooms," she said as they walked downstairs. "They're nice. Very girly. You'd be uncomfortable."

"On many levels," he said.

She laughed, then pointed. "Reception. The trainers have that office. There's a lounge with vending machines. I've been approached by a couple of juice bar companies, but I can't decide if I want to get into that or not."

She led the way down a short hall that ended at a colorful aquatic mural surrounding glass doors with a view to a bright and cheerful day care center.

"This is what makes me happy," she said. "When I started my first gym, I wanted to make day care a priority. It took some doing, but we have a center in each of our gyms. There are a couple of unique features.

First, any member can use the day care center while we're open for up to four hours a day. We charge a very nominal fee for that, which means Mom can drop off her kids if she has an unexpected appointment, or needs to run a couple of errands. Or even if she needs some sanity time."

He frowned. "Aren't you overrun with kids?"

"Almost never. Our members appreciate the service and don't take advantage of it in a bad way. It's something I wanted to do and it's working. We also have a very high ratio of child-care providers to kids."

He looked into the center and saw she was right. Most of the kids were one-on-one with an adult.

"The local community colleges and the state college all have child care majors," she said. "I'm an official member of their program, which means college kids can get their internship credits here. I work with their schedules and they love me. I always have a licensed professional on duty, but the majority of the help is provided by the students. They're young and energetic and enthused. It's a win-win for everyone."

He turned his attention from the day care center to the woman standing next to him. She was nothing like Stacey, which wasn't good or bad. Just an interesting fact. Two weeks ago, he would have sworn he would never be interested in another woman ever. Now he wasn't so sure.

"You're saving the world," he said.

She laughed. "Oh, please. I'm desperately trying to affect one tiny corner."

"Which you're doing."

"I try. It's funny. I majored in finance when I was in college and got a job with a money management firm after I graduated. Within the first year, I knew I'd made a desperate mistake. I hated what I did, I missed playing sports and hanging out with my girlfriends all the time. I wanted to be on a team, but not the corporate one I'd signed up for. I was totally miserable."

She shrugged. "One day a client came in. She had a small gym and wasn't making it. She wanted to talk to me about filing for bankruptcy. As I listened to her, I felt as if I'd been hit by lightning. I knew I wanted to buy that gym. I believed I could make it successful. I wanted gyms all over Riverside and beyond."

"Which you made happen."

She looked at him. "I worked my butt off and it was so worth it. Even when I was scared, I never regretted my decision. Now I have everything I want." She paused. "Almost everything."

He wondered what was missing.

"I get buyout offers all the time," she told him. "I always say no, but I'm willing to admit I love being asked."

She was vibrant and alive and that energy rubbed off on him. He hated having to check his watch and didn't like the time when he saw it.

She caught his action. "You have to go."

"Sorry. I'm meeting a family to discuss treatment options."

"That can't be fun."

He shrugged. "I always hope for a miracle and some-times I get it."

"Which makes it a good day."

"Agreed." He stared into her eyes and felt that connection again. He wanted her, which also felt good. This living thing had a lot to say for itself. "I want to see you again," he told her.

She hesitated, then smiled. "I wouldn't mind being seen."

"I'll call."

"Guys always say that."

"You think I'm just some guy?" he asked playfully.

"I haven't decided."

"You'll let me know when you do?"

"You'll be the first."

The design for the dollhouse had looked easy enough, Josh thought as he sanded the edges of the individual roof shingles so Emma wouldn't get splinters. He and Pete had picked it out together and figured it would take them two, maybe three weekends, tops.

That had been several months ago. Originally planned as Emma's Christmas present, the brothers were now determined to finish it for her birthday. Or at least before she stopped playing with dolls.

"What did you think of Crissy?" Pete asked as he primed the shutters Josh had sanded in preparation for paint. "Abbey and I both liked her. She did good with all the kids. She was here for lunch with Abbey and the kids a couple of days ago and Abbey said it went well."

Josh hesitated, not sure what he wanted to admit to his brother. Then he reminded himself that he and Pete had never kept secrets.

"She mentioned that when I stopped by her gym to see her."

Pete put down his brush and stared. "You stopped by? To talk to her? On purpose?"

"You're dripping." Josh pointed to the primer collecting on the end of the bristles.

Pete swore under his breath and grabbed the brush. "You're seeing her? I know Abbey was pushing something, but I didn't think you were interested."

"I wasn't. I'm not." He shook his head. Who was he trying to kid? "I might be interested. We're friends."

Friends who slept together. If only he could forget that night…and morning…he'd spent with her.

But a part of him didn't want to forget. A part of him wanted to do it again.

Pete tossed a rag at him. "Where'd you go?"

"What? Just thinking."

"About Crissy?" Pete sounded shocked and intrigued. "You like her."

"I think she's great."

"So you're considering dating her?" Pete grinned as he asked the question.

"Maybe." Did dating describe what he and Crissy were doing? Had done?

"Come on. It'll be good for you. You need to get out and do something other than work and hang out here."

Josh picked up another shingle and began sanding it. "Trying to get rid of me?"

"I'm trying to remind you that you're still alive. I know you loved Stacey and that you want to honor her memory, but barely existing doesn't honor anyone. You live like a monk or worse. Get out there. Date. Have sex. You're putting too much pressure on yourself. You weren't meant to live like this, Josh."

"So speaks a guy who has had exactly one woman in his life."

Pete's expression turned smug. "Why go looking for more when you have the best at home? But we're not talking about me. We're talking about you. Use it or lose it, my friend."

Josh concentrated on the shingle, smoothing the edges and the top. "I did use it. Last week."

He kept his attention on his work but heard the satisfying *splat* of the brush hitting the floor, followed by creative swearing.

"What?" Pete demanded. "You did it? With a woman?"

"I'm ignoring you."

"Seriously. Who—" Pete paused, then swore again. "Crissy?"

Josh finally looked at his older brother and shrugged. As if it wasn't a big deal and something he hadn't been able to get out of his mind for more than five minutes at a time.

"I went to her house after the party to make sure she was all right. She wasn't. One thing led to another."

Pete looked impressed. "When you cut loose, you do it in a big way." Then his expression turned serious. "How'd you feel the next morning?"

"Better than I thought I would," he admitted, remembering how he'd expected guilt and remorse. "I expected to feel like crap and I didn't. I didn't plan on healing but it happened anyway."

"Is that a bad thing?"

"I don't want to lose Stacey."

"She's already gone."

Josh knew that in his head, but in his gut, he wasn't so sure. "I thought she'd be a part of me forever. I have the memories, but she's not inside of me anymore. Every part of me says it's time to move on, to get a life, but I'm not sure I want to. Or that I should. How can I have let go of Stacey so easily?"

"It's been four years. That's not easy." Pete shook his head. "You loved her and you lost her. That doesn't mean you can't get involved again with someone else."

Josh hadn't thought in terms of getting involved. He liked Crissy. He enjoyed being with her, in and out of bed. He'd never thought he'd be aroused again, or excited about seeing a woman who wasn't Stacey. But getting involved? That was a place he didn't want to go.

"I'm not interested in anything serious," he said.

"No one's asking you to marry her," Pete pointed out. "Date her. Dating can be fun. Enjoy what you have. Remember what it was like not to feel so dead inside. That's allowed. As to the rest of it, you can make it up as you go."

Josh eyed his brother. "You've been with Abbey since you were fourteen or fifteen. How can you know all this stuff?"

"I'm gifted," Pete said modestly, then laughed. "The guys at the fire station talk. The single ones talk the most. I listen. You like Crissy. She likes you, which makes me wonder how smart she is, but that's a different discussion."

"Thanks," Josh grumbled, enjoying his brother's teasing.

"So go for it. Enjoy what you have with her."

It sounded like a plan, Josh thought. As long as they were both clear on the fact that his relationship with Crissy wasn't going anywhere. He was willing to like her and want her, but he would never love her. He'd already given his heart once—to Stacey—and he was never going to risk losing it again.

Chapter Six

Crissy ran the cloth ribbon across the back of the sofa. King Edward, her cat, blinked at her as if asking why she didn't have something better to do with her Saturday afternoon than annoy him.

"You can't sleep all day long," she told him.

He slowly closed his eyes as if to prove her wrong.

She stood and paced the length of the living room. She felt restless, which was unusual for her. An afternoon at home was always something she looked forward to. She worked hard at her job during the week and solitary time was precious. Normally she savored a couple of hours spent reading a book or watching a movie she'd missed when it was out in theaters.

But not today. Today she couldn't seem to settle on anything.

"I should go shopping," she told herself, but felt no call of the mall. And if she wasn't compelled by trying on shoes she didn't need then there really *was* something wrong with her.

The "what" wasn't too hard to figure out. Josh and the complications he'd brought into her life.

She'd kind of fooled herself into thinking she was doing a lovely job of ignoring him right up until he'd shown up at her office. Having him in her face had destroyed the illusion.

Now she was left with reality, which wasn't pretty. She was obsessed with a man possibly still in love with his dead wife. The same man was also the uncle of the child she'd given up for adoption and there was a teeny, tiny chance she might be pregnant with his child.

Any number of TV channels would probably be willing to pay a fortune for the chance to fictionalize her current situation. Not that much fiction would be required. It was kind of dramatic all on its own.

Which did not make for a calm Saturday afternoon.

She crossed to the calendar in the kitchen and studied the date. She would be able to take a pregnancy test in less than two weeks. That wasn't so long. She could survive that time. And honestly, the odds of the whole sperm-egg encounter were infinitesimal…weren't they?

The phone rang.

Crissy hated that her first thought/hope was that it was Josh, which made her feel sixteen again. Not really a good thing.

"Hello?"

"Hi, Crissy."

It *was* Josh. Heat flooded her body and her chest tightened, making it difficult to breathe, but in a good way.

"I just finished up working on a dollhouse for Emma," he continued. "Pete and I have been building it for months and we're down to the painting. We want to have it finished for her birthday."

"I'm sure she'll love it."

Emma seemed very girly, Crissy thought. She would have hated a dollhouse at the same age.

"Me, too," he said. "At least Pete and I have been spending a lot of time together. That doesn't always happen."

"You're both busy."

She sank into a kitchen chair and wondered if he had a point to his call. Anticipation kept trying to get out but, as she wasn't sure if there was anything to anticipate or if this was just a chance to talk, she kept slamming the door.

"I'm calling to invite you to dinner," he said. "Tonight."

Anticipation rushed out and started dancing.

She opened, then closed her mouth. What was she supposed to say? Yes made the most sense, but did she want to do this? Date Josh?

She liked him a lot, but there were issues and she'd always found issue-based relationships were nothing but trouble.

"Did I violate the dating code?" he asked.

"What?"

"It's last minute. I should have called a few days ago. I'm not good at dating. Lack of practice. Not to mention that you don't want to date me."

"I never said that."

"You said we should just be friends. Sort of the same thing."

"If you're going to be logical," she grumbled as she picked up a pen and began doodling on a paper napkin. "It's not that I don't like you."

"Would you be more comfortable going out with me if you disliked me?" he asked.

She smiled. "No. The liking is a good thing."

"I like you, too."

Her insides got all warm.

Crissy sucked in a breath. They both knew all the reasons getting involved wasn't really smart. They'd been over them more than once. But she couldn't stop thinking about him and apparently he had her on the brain, too. Honestly, how often did she meet a guy she thought was special?

"I'm offering to cook," he said.

"You know how?"

"I can pull a few things together. Two or three."

"That's more than I can do," she said, smiling. "I'm the takeout queen. But I have lovely dishes. I can make takeout look pretty."

"Something to be proud of. Are you impressed enough to say yes?"

She wanted to. Desperately. In a way, that kind of scared her. Caring about Josh too much could be dangerous for her reluctant heart. But saying no seemed as if it could hurt more.

"Are we dating?" she asked. "Is this dating?"

"It might be. Although given what happened the other night, probably not a first date."

She laughed. "Good. I loathe first dates. They're always so awkward. Let's never have a first date."

"You have my word on it."

She drew in a breath. "What time?"

"Seven."

"I'll be there."

"I'll look forward to seeing you."

Crissy had no idea what to wear. The dinner was at Josh's house, which meant more casual was probably better. But jeans seemed too casual, a dress seemed too formal. The weather was clear and in the mid-sixties—fairly typical for Riverside this time of year. After flipping through every item in her closet three times, she settled on a sweater with a sweetheart neckline and slim black pants.

She went light on the makeup and fluffed her hair. With everything done, she glanced at the clock and realized she had plenty of time to be nervous. Maybe she should leave now and stop at the wine store on her way. She always liked to bring something when she was invited to dinner.

Three minutes after she was due to arrive, she parked in front of Josh's town house and turned off the engine. Anticipation mingled with apprehension. It was an uneasy mixture at best. She grabbed her purse and the wine she'd bought, then got out of the car and headed for the front door.

He opened the door before she could knock and smiled.

"Thanks for coming," he said as he stepped back to let her inside.

At the sight of him, the soulful green eyes, the familiar curve of his mouth, the white shirt that covered a chest she remembered really, really well, she felt her knees go weak.

"My pleasure," she murmured, stepping into the small foyer. "Are you really cooking or is there takeout involved? I'm just asking. I totally respect takeout."

"I'm cooking." He shrugged. "Barbecuing, which is almost the same thing."

She laughed. "Okay. I feel better now. Meat on fire is a traditional male dish. I was afraid you were using pots and pans and sautéing things. That would have been intimidating."

"I wouldn't want that."

She handed him the wine. He took it then leaned in and kissed her. On the mouth.

It was a slow, lingering kiss. He didn't push. Instead the warm brush of his mouth seemed to…promise good things to come. In the battle of emotions, it appeared anticipation might win.

She put her hand on his shoulder. His strength made her think that maybe it was okay not to be in charge all the time, that this might be a man more interested in being a partner than someone she had to take care of.

The thought was so startling, she stepped back, then fumbled with her purse to buy herself time to recover.

"Where should I put this?" she asked, glancing around the empty foyer.

"There's a table in the living room." He put his hand on the small of her back and urged her forward.

What was up with the idea of Josh as a partner?

Because he was strong? She didn't get involved with weak men. Okay, sure, there had been a couple of disasters, but she'd been dating since she was sixteen. In over fifteen years, there were bound to be a few mistakes. But it wasn't as if she had a pattern of choosing men who were weaker than herself, was it?

"Are you all right?" Josh asked.

"What? Oh. I'm fine. Just thinking about something weird." She consciously cleared her mind. "I'm totally focused on the moment now. Color me here."

"Good."

He led her into a large room that was nearly painful in its sterility. The walls were builder's white, the carpet a nondescript beige. There was a big TV, a sofa, love seat and several tables with lamps. The furniture coordinated so perfectly she had a bad feeling he'd bought them off the showroom floor of some discount furniture place.

Despite the excess of seating, there was nothing personal in the space. No pictures or plants, no artwork. Not even a magazine.

She set her purse in the corner of the love seat and glanced at the vertical blinds covering the sliding glass door leading out to an enclosed patio. Obviously Josh had moved here after Stacey had died.

"You had a house together, didn't you?" she asked without thinking.

He frowned. "Yes. How did you…" He looked at the room, then at her. "That obvious?"

"Probably not. I'm especially perceptive. Although a case could be made that the lack of anything personal sort of gives it all away."

He gave her a smile that didn't reach his eyes. "You're right." He shrugged. "The house was great but after Stacey was gone, I couldn't stay there. I sold it and gave our furniture to a shelter. It was easier than trying to live there."

"I've never lost anyone," she admitted. "I don't know what it's like to go through that much pain. I didn't mean to make things worse by mentioning the house."

He met her gaze. "You didn't. It was four years ago."

Was that his way of saying he'd moved on? She wanted to think so, but wasn't sure.

"Come on," he said, taking her hand. "You'll like the kitchen. There's color in there."

"How did that happen?"

"Builder error. One of my neighbors special-ordered tile, cabinets and wall color. They put it in here by mistake. As none of it could be easily removed, I decided to live with it."

They walked into a room done in Mediterranean colors. The tiles were shades of cream with an ocean-blue backsplash. Graduated shades of yellow warmed the walls. The cabinets were a slick, shiny dark red.

When compared with the starkness of the rest of the place, it seemed as if they'd stepped into another house.

"I love it," she said as she turned slowly to take it all in. "Did the other people get their kitchen redone the way they wanted?"

"Not exactly. When they found out what had happened, they came over to check out my place and decided it was a little too bright for their taste."

"Fools," she murmured, then walked over to the

cooktop. "Not a single burner in use. I feel more comfortable now."

"We're having cold salads with our steaks," he said.

She opened her eyes wide. "Steaks? Josh, I own gyms. I'm totally into healthy foods. I don't eat meat."

His face took on a "damn, I've seriously screwed up" expression. Crissy did her best not to look anything but horrified. Then his gaze narrowed.

"You ate hot dogs at the party at Pete's house," he said. "I saw you."

She laughed. "I know. I love steak. I was just trying to mess with your head."

"It worked." He put the bottle of wine on the center island and nodded to one of the stools. "My mother would love you."

"Really? She likes women who torment her sons?"

He began to open the bottle. "She likes smart women who don't take a lot of crap from men. Interesting considering her father is a general and my father is an executive. His job took us around the world. Pete and I grew up in Europe and Asia. It gave us a different perspective."

"In what way?"

"Mom has causes. She loves causes. Everything from save the whales to helping women start their own businesses. The cause changed with our location, but not her dedication. We learned early to work to make a difference."

It might seem strange that two guys who could live anywhere would choose to settle here, Crissy thought. But maybe not. She had a feeling the brothers had deliberately chosen to be close to each other, to stay connected. As for causes, each had chosen a profession designed to save people.

"Where are your parents now?" she asked.

"Italy. It's their favorite place and they're considering retiring there."

"I thought my parents were far away in Florida," she said. "Do you wish they were closer?"

"Sometimes." He poured them each a glass of wine, then passed her one. "They're good people, but not exactly connected as parents. They were always more interested in what they were doing than us."

Which explained why he and Pete were so close.

"You came back to the U.S. for college?" she asked.

He nodded. "I'd always wanted to. I knew I wanted to be a doctor, so that part was easy. Pete knew what he wanted, too. My parents tried to talk him out of being a firefighter, but he wouldn't listen."

"So you're both stubborn," she teased.

"Focused."

"Uh-huh." She sipped her wine. "So how did you meet Stacey?"

She hadn't meant to ask the question. It had just slipped out. She half expected Josh to refuse to answer. Instead he leaned against the counter and smiled.

"I was doing rotations. You spend a certain amount of time in different parts of the hospital, learning about each one. I'd asked for pediatrics and ended up in pediatric oncology. I didn't want to be there. A bunch of dying kids seemed too depressing, but I quickly got there was so much hope on the ward. One day Stacey dropped by to visit some kids."

He gazed just past her but she had a feeling he was seeing a different time and place. And a different woman.

"She didn't know anyone in the hospital. She'd just dropped by to visit because she wanted to brighten some kid's day. She asked the nurse who was getting visited the least and settled in for a long afternoon of talking and playing. The patient was a little girl named Wendy. I walked in on Stacey painting Wendy's toenails purple."

There was something in his voice, Crissy realized. A quality of love and respect that made her feel as if she'd accidentally burst in on a private moment.

"They were both laughing. I thought Stacey was her sister. I wanted to talk about Wendy's condition with a family member. Stacey told me who she was and we ended up going for coffee." He shook his head. "She was so beautiful. I couldn't speak in whole sentences without stuttering around her. She was bright and funny. I asked her out and she told me she had six months to live."

Crissy stiffened. "She was dying?"

"She was joking. She explained she'd had cancer as a kid and it was the kind that usually came back. She teased she could be dead by morning. Or in forty years. But she knew there was a time bomb buried inside of her."

Crissy wished she hadn't asked the question. What had she been thinking? Or had she been hoping that there was a massive flaw in Josh's late wife? Something that would make her believe that he was over Stacey?

"I didn't care," he continued. "I wanted whatever time there was. She kept putting me off, but eventually

I wore her down. We started dating. When I proposed, we went through the whole thing again. She didn't want to tie me down to someone who could get sick at any moment. I didn't want to live without her."

He glanced at her. "Is this more information than you wanted?"

"No," she said automatically, even though it was.

Part of the problem wasn't the words, but how he said them. Love thickened his voice, making her aware that he was still very much in love with his late wife. It also made her wonder if any part of his pursuit of Stacey had been because she was safe. There was a finite quality to their relationship that most people didn't have. Then she told herself she was searching for demons where they didn't exist.

"It took nine months of me begging, but she finally agreed to marry me," he said. "We had almost four years." He frowned. "She's been gone longer than we were married. I never thought of it that way before."

"Did you pick your specialty because of her?"

"She was part of the reason, but mostly it was the kids I met on my rotation. I wanted to save them all. I was arrogant enough to think I could."

"Were you wrong?"

His eyes darkened. "Sometimes."

"You keep putting my life in perspective," she admitted, still uncomfortable with the intensity of the conversation. "I don't really have the right to complain about anything."

"Don't say that. We all deal with stuff. It's relative. Just because you're not facing a life-threatening illness doesn't mean you can't worry about what's happening in your life."

"Is that what you tell yourself?" she asked.

"I try."

"Does it work?"

"Not when I have a sick kid in my office."

"You worry about what's important," she said. "Maybe that's a better use of our time. Maybe we should all remember not to sweat the small stuff."

"I'm not sure those lessons last," he said, then straightened. "Okay. This isn't what I'd thought we'd be talking about. Change of topic here. How was traffic?"

She smiled. "There wasn't any."

He walked around the island and took her hand. "Come on. I'll show you my barbecue. It's big and manly. You'll be impressed."

"I'm sure I will be."

She appreciated that he was trying to lighten the mood. Crissy didn't want to spend the evening talking about or even thinking about Josh's late wife. Yet in some ways Stacey was there, with them.

She was the absence of life in the town house, the reason Josh hadn't been out with a woman in years. She was the ghost who was never far from his thoughts.

What had Stacey been like? A saint? Or just a regular person? How was she, Crissy, different and how was she the same?

As they walked out onto the patio, she wondered what would happen if she really *was* pregnant. Would Josh want to embrace a new life or was he too deeply stuck in the past?

What about her own feelings? He was a great guy and she sensed a lot of potential between them. But was she willing to trust her heart to someone who might still be in love with someone else?

Brandon was already a complication and a baby would just make things worse.

There wasn't a baby, she reminded herself. There couldn't be. As if willing it so would change anything.

After dinner they moved back into the living room. Josh put on an instrumental CD, then joined Crissy on the sofa. The steaks had turned out well, she'd seemed to like the salad selection he'd provided. So far his first dinner at home was going well.

He'd wondered if the evening would be awkward. Except for Pete helping him install his large television, he hadn't had anyone over to the place. He barely spent any time there himself. He was usually working long hours or hanging out at Pete and Abbey's house. The town house was where he slept and kept his clothes. It wasn't home. He hadn't had a home since Stacey died.

Stacey. He hadn't meant to talk about her so much earlier. Despite the potential for disaster, Crissy hadn't run screaming into the night, so that was something.

Now she tossed her head as she looked around the room. The light caught the colors in her hair and illuminated her beautiful face.

"I can't stand it," she said. "You need some stuff in this room."

"Stuff?"

"Magazines, books, pictures on the wall. A throw."

"Guys don't have throws."

"I could knit you one. Maybe. Probably. Then it would be a gift rather than a decorator piece."

He liked the idea of her making something for him. "You've told me about your knitting ability," he teased. "Would I know it was a throw?"

She wrinkled her nose. "I'm not *that* horrible." She sighed. "Actually I am, so maybe a throw isn't a good idea. But you need something bright and cheery in this room. Something personal. Although I'm totally the wrong person to be giving advice. Now Noelle has a great house. It's perfectly decorated. Of course Dev, her husband, used a decorator before he met Noelle. So you need a decorator."

"No, thanks."

She leaned toward him. "It's because you're afraid, isn't it?"

"I want to be comfortable in my house."

"The assumption being you wouldn't be comfortable?"

"I'm not into little animal statues on coffee tables."

She laughed. "Me, either. But I love the theory. Noelle has all those female talents. She's done a great job in the baby's room. I've told you she's seriously pregnant, right?"

"You mentioned it."

"She's going to pop in the next couple of weeks. Her baby shower is tomorrow. I can't wait. I don't actually like showers, but I'm compelled to attend them. It's the delicious food and really fun, if weird, games."

He'd never been to a shower of any kind. "You play games?"

"Uh-huh. You'd hate them. So girly. And there's usually a color scheme and the drinks and mints and napkins all match. I'm guessing with Noelle and Dev knowing they're having a girl, everything will be pink."

She looked delighted. A baby shower sounded like his idea of hell, but then he wasn't female.

"Have fun," he told her.

"We will."

She smiled at him and something shifted inside him. Something hot and hard and hungry.

It must have shown because her eyebrows raised as she asked, "What are you thinking?"

"Nothing in particular."

"I find that hard to believe. You must be thinking something."

Rather than explain, he leaned across the distance between them and kissed her. At the same time, he buried his hand in her hair, letting the soft, silky strands slip through his fingers. She wrapped both her arms around his neck and melted into him.

Her body had started to become familiar to him. He could anticipate the combination of curves and soft skin settling against him. Blood pooled in his groin, making him hard in an instant.

As much as he wanted to take her right there on the sofa, he enjoyed the waiting nearly as much. Knowing what would happen when he took her to bed, how she would look at him, how her breathing would quicken, her body would writhe, all added to the moment. He would take it slow tonight—all the better to please both of them.

* * *

Crissy let herself get lost in Josh's kiss. She hadn't been sure she was ready for them to make love again. They hadn't defined their relationship, nor did she know if she was pregnant or not. Still, now that she was here, in his arms, she didn't want to stop. There was something about the man that made her weak in the knees.

She parted her lips to let him sweep inside. He tasted of the wine they'd had at dinner. As his tongue circled hers, she felt her body flushing. Heat poured into her belly, then slipped lower, making her ready.

He shifted his hand toward her breasts. She tensed in anticipation. But just as they were about to get to the good part, he pulled back, then stood and drew her to her feet.

"We'll be more comfortable upstairs," he murmured, then pressed his lips against the side of her neck.

She tingled where his mouth touched her. While the sensible part of her brain knew that a bed made a lot more sense than a sofa, the eager, swollen woman bits were anxious to get the party started.

Still, when he stepped back and took her hand, she followed him willingly.

The upstairs was as plain as the downstairs. Crissy caught sight of a hall bathroom and an open door to what looked like a home office. Then Josh led her through open double doors into a spacious master bedroom with a king-size bed.

The only light spilled in from the hallway. The rest of the furniture was in shadow, which she didn't mind. The bed was the only piece that interested her.

She kicked off her shoes before turning to him. He pulled her against him and kissed her mouth. Once again she welcomed him inside, loving the feel of his tongue against hers.

They moved eagerly, but with a rhythm that made her feel as if they were meant to be lovers. Just as she thought about pulling off her sweater, he tugged at the hem. She reached for the buttons on his shirt the exact moment he began tugging it from his waistband.

Slacks and socks and panties and briefs followed until they were both naked, but still standing. Then Josh broke their kisses and dropped to his knees in front of her.

"You're so beautiful," he whispered as he kissed his way across her belly. "Everything about you gets to me."

His mouth was warm and erotic. He used his tongue to draw circles on her skin. His hands slipped up and down the backs of her thighs. Then he slipped around to the front of her legs and eased toward the apex of her legs. Before she'd figured out what he was doing, he parted her curls, leaned in and licked the very core of her.

She sucked in a breath, then groaned in perfect pleasure as he played with her. He circled and brushed, then sucked until she began to tremble. Heat poured through her. She wanted to spread her legs more and beg him to take her to climax. She wanted to hang on to something so she wouldn't fall. She was off balance and aroused and terrified he would stop what he was doing before she was done.

But he didn't stop. He stroked her over and over again until she couldn't think about anything but how good he made her feel. Still touching her with his lips and his tongue, he urged her backward.

She took one step, then another, until she felt the bed behind her. She sat, then lay back and drew her legs as far apart as they would go. Her feet didn't touch the ground, but that hardly mattered. Not as long as Josh knelt there, pleasing her with his hot, wet caress.

He shifted slightly, then stretched out his arms until his hands closed on her breasts. He rubbed her curves before lightly brushing her tight nipples with his fingertips.

It was too much, she thought hazily. Too much pleasure, too much sensation. Tension built until it filled every part of her. She drew back her knees, exposing herself more, then grabbed onto the bedspread in an attempt to hold out for a couple more seconds.

It was too late. Her climax shuddered through her, making her cry out as the wonder of it filled every cell. She lost herself in the pleasure of her body responding to his touch. Ripples of release went on and on until they finally slowed and she could breathe again.

Only then did Josh move to her thigh and kiss her lightly. He moved his hands to her side. She straightened her legs and let her feet dangle. Finally she opened her eyes.

"Amazing," she said, then laughed at how low and froggy her voice sounded.

"You liked it?"

She raised herself on one elbow and looked at him. "You're kidding, right? You have to ask?"

"A guy likes a little flattery."

"You make love like you mean it and speaking as the

recipient, I'm incredibly grateful. And relaxed. I think entire body parts melted."

He chuckled. "Nice flattery."

"I wasn't kidding."

He stood and stretched. She took a moment to admire his erection and anticipate what it would feel like buried deep inside of her. Her belly clenched.

He lowered his arms and looked at her. "Like I said before. Beautiful."

She shifted back on the bed to make room for him. "Thank you."

He bent down to his nightstand, opened a drawer and pulled out a condom.

For a second she wondered if it was too little, too late, but decided not to go there. "Are they new?" she asked.

He shrugged. "Yes. I should have thought of them before. It's just…"

She knew what it had been. Four years of abstinence after losing his wife. Why would he be traveling with protection? She's the one who should have thought of it. Only Josh had caught her unawares, in more ways than one.

She smiled. "Okay, big guy. Put on a cowboy hat and let's party."

He knelt on the bed, then slipped on his condom. "You do have a way with words."

"I'm charming."

"Yes, you are."

He shifted between her legs and stared into her eyes as he slowly, deliberately, moved inside of her.

He filled her completely, stretching her, making her breath catch. Despite her recent release, the feel of him made her hungry again. She wrapped her legs around his hips and ran her hands down his back.

He shuddered. "You're a temptation."

"So are you."

He withdrew, only to push in again. With each thrust, she tensed and wanted more. She sensed he was holding back.

"More," she murmured, still holding his gaze and watching the need dilate his eyes. "You don't have to hold back."

"I don't want to hurt you."

"You won't."

He hesitated for a second. She gave a little thrust with her hips to urge him on. Apparently taking her at her word, he pushed in hard, faster, filling her until she wanted to scream, then pulled out again. He moved with purpose and she felt the exact moment he lost control.

His eyes closed and his face tightened. His body tensed and he took her with a force that pushed her over the edge to her own release. Seconds after her muscles began to convulse, he cried out, then shuddered and they were lost together.

Later, when he was asleep, Crissy listened to the sound of his breathing and wondered if she was in danger of getting in too deep with this man. Was there still time to protect her heart or had she fallen so far, so fast, there was no going back?

Chapter Seven

Crissy still hummed with contentment from her activities the previous night. She parked on the street by Noelle's house, collected the large teddy-bear-topped package containing her gift of adorable dresses for the well-dressed newborn through two-year-old girl and stepped out of her car. She saw Rachel and waved.

"How are you feeling?" she called.

Rachel touched her stomach. "Good. I'm going to take notes so that when I have my shower, I know what to register for."

Crissy laughed. "Are you seriously worried?"

"No. Carter and his family will make sure I'm well taken care of." Rachel looked happy as she spoke, as if she was confident that the Brockett clan would look out for her.

Crissy hugged her friend, then linked arms as they walked up to the large, beautiful house.

"When I marry a millionaire," Crissy said, "I want a house just like this."

Rachel grinned. "You won't have to marry a millionaire. You'll make your own millions. You probably already have."

"Not technically," Crissy said. "I live modestly."

"More modestly than you have to?"

"Maybe."

The gyms were doing well. Crissy probably could afford a bigger place, but right now she was in grow-the-business mode. All her spare cash went back into her work. If she was pregnant, that might have to change.

Not that she was. Denying the possibility was her new plan. It made things much easier.

"You're not going to see me on the Fortune 500 list anytime soon," she said.

"But one day," Rachel told her. "I used to think I'd be all about my career. Maybe switch from teaching to administration, but now I don't think so."

"Too focused on the baby?"

"Yes," Rachel admitted. "I'm not sure I'm even going to come back after my maternity leave. Is that too traditional? Do you hate me for that?"

"Why would I hate you?" Crissy asked. "We can want different things and still be friends."

"I know, but sometimes, when I look at all you've done, I feel like a slacker."

"You're not." Crissy knew she was totally intent on her career. It had been more satisfying than the disaster

that had been her personal life. Maybe all that was about
to change. Not that she would give up work, but a little
more balance could be a good thing.

"What did you get for the baby?" Rachel asked.

"Impractically beautiful dresses. A couple for each
size between newborn and age two. I meant to be more
sensible, but when I saw those tiny dresses, I couldn't
help myself."

"Sounds more fun than the month of diaper service
I got," Rachel said, waving an envelope. "Noelle said
she wanted to avoid disposable diapers as much as
possible. I'm being supportive."

"She'll love it. Plus, your gift makes more sense.
Honestly, who puts a newborn in a fancy dress?"

Rachel laughed. "Noelle will. You know she will. If
the baby has hair, she'll put in coordinating bows. If the
baby doesn't, they'll be stuck on somehow."

Crissy chuckled at the thought and knew Rachel was
right.

"I'm not the least bit maternal," she murmured more
to herself than Rachel. "That could be a problem."

"You have other skills," Rachel said as they approached the front door. "But I know what you mean.
I worry about the baby stage. Give me a four-year-old
and I'm totally comfortable, but the floppy months
make me really nervous."

"Carter will be there to help."

"And his mother and sisters." Rachel sounded delighted by the fact. "They have a lot of expertise. I know
all I'll have to do is call and help will be there."

The front door open. Dev waved them in.

"Family room," he said. "Only two more arrivals and then I get to leave."

"All these women making you nervous?" Crissy asked, enjoying the sight of the always in-control Dev looking harried.

"You have no idea. Everything is pink. I half expected Noelle's mother to want to paint the family room pink so it would match."

Crissy had the thought that Dev and Josh would get along. They had similar sensibilities. Maybe, after the baby was born, the four of them could go out sometime. She looked at Rachel. Maybe the six of them.

"You came," a very pregnant Noelle called from her place of honor in an overstuffed chair by the window. "I was getting worried."

"No, you weren't," Crissy said as she walked over, bent down and hugged her.

"Okay, not really," Noelle admitted. "I knew you wouldn't miss my shower."

"How could we? We've been involved from the beginning. We love you too much not to be there at the end."

"That's right," Rachel said, moving in for her hug. "I believe I was the one telling you to go for it, where Dev was concerned."

"You were both worried about me and I love you for it." Noelle sniffed. "Oh, no. Hormones. Quick. Say something funny so I don't start to cry."

"Carter's mom wants me to name the baby Hortense, if it's a girl. Apparently it's a family name."

Noelle giggled. "Hortense? Seriously? You wouldn't do that to an innocent child, would you?"

"I wouldn't want to," Rachel told her with a grin. "But we'll have to see how labor goes. I've been telling my stomach that for the past couple of days. If things go smoothly, you can have a cool name. But stick me with forty-eight hours of screaming you might be known as Hortense…even if you *are* a boy."

Crissy left them alone to drop her present off in the impressive pile by the coffee table, then went into the kitchen to see if she could help.

Noelle's mother greeted her, then motioned to the hardworking women who seemed to have everything under control.

"I'm impressed," Crissy said. "My party-hosting skills are limited to an opening I did for my last gym. I hired caterers. My big involvement was writing a check."

"You forget I'm a minister's wife. I can do this sort of thing in my sleep. How's Noelle holding up?"

"She's a little emotional, but happy. We're all anxious for the baby to be born."

"I agree." Noelle's mother sighed. "When I first heard she'd married Dev to give the baby a name, I thought she was on the road to disaster. But everything turned out more wonderful than I could have imagined. Now I'm going to be a grandmother."

Crissy knew Noelle's mother was barely in her forties. "Are you okay with that? I mean, you're kind of young."

"My baby's having a baby. That's pretty cool." She squeezed Crissy's arm. "You'll see what I mean when you start having babies yourself. I know it sounds silly, but there's something powerful about watching the next generation being born. It anchors my place in the universe. Does that make sense?"

Crissy nodded, even though she wasn't sure she understood. She tried to imagine Brandon old enough to get married and have children. How would she feel about that?

But instead of seeing the future, she felt a wave of longing and a sense of having missed something important. Something amazing. However much she and Brandon became friends now, she would never be his mother. The time lost was gone forever. His bond with Abbey and Pete was unshakable, and in truth she, Crissy, didn't want to upset that. But there was a sense of emptiness inside of her she'd never experienced before.

Twelve years ago she'd gained the freedom she'd wanted, but at what price?

Crissy celebrated finding a new, reliable cleaning service for her gyms by ordering a nonfat blueberry muffin with her usual lunch salad. When she returned to her office, it was to find a phone message from Josh.

Her insides actually quivered when she heard his voice.

"Hi, Crissy. It's Josh. Give me a call when you get a chance. I have a proposition for you."

She lived with the anticipation for a couple of minutes before calling him back. Anticipation turned to pleasure when the receptionist said, "He's been waiting for your call. I'll put you right through."

Seconds later Josh came on the line. "Where were you?" he asked. "Hanging out with some buff guys who can bench press four-fifty?"

"Only on alternate Wednesdays," she teased. Was it possible he wondered about how she spent her day and worried about someone else catching her attention? He always seemed so perfectly together and confident. It was nice to think he was in over his head, too.

"So I won't ask again until next week."

She heard the humor in his voice.

"What's up?" she asked. "You mentioned a proposition. Or was that just cheap talk?"

"Not talk. I'm going to be getting a puppy tomorrow afternoon. I thought you might want to come with me."

"A puppy." She tried to picture one in his all-white town house. "Most guys start with a plant."

"It's not for me. Alicia, one of my patients, is turning ten. She wasn't expected to make it past her eighth birthday. She's been cancer free for eighteen months and her parents want to give her a puppy. She wants me to pick it out."

"That's a lot of responsibility."

"Less than it sounds. Her parents took her to a breeder, where they narrowed it down to three puppies. The breeder has been watching them for the past couple of days to see which one would be best with her. All I have to do is go pick it up and deliver it. I thought maybe you'd like to come along."

Puppy shopping, huh? Was there any other activity designed to show a woman a guy's softer side? Was she already at risk where Josh was concerned? Yet she couldn't figure out a good reason to say no.

"I'd like that," she said. "What time?"

* * *

Crissy was waiting for Josh in the foyer of her gym. It probably wasn't cool, but she was too excited to wait upstairs. What was it about puppies, kittens and babies that made a person crazy? Not that she was as excited about the puppy as she was about seeing Josh.

She saw him pull up in an SUV she'd seen parked at Pete and Abbey's house and grinned as she opened the passenger's door.

"So we don't want to risk puppy piddle in our fancy doctor car," she teased by way of greeting.

He gave her a half smile that didn't reach his eyes, then leaned over and lightly kissed her cheek. "It was Pete's idea. I didn't say no."

She stared at him, taking in the shadowed hollowness of his face. It was as if something had sucked the life out of him.

"Josh, what's wrong?" she asked, thinking of Brandon and praying he was all right.

"Nothing. I'm fine."

"Are you sure? Abbey and the kids are okay? Pete?"

He frowned. "They're all good. Why?"

"You look different. Something happened."

He put the SUV in Drive and turned onto the street. After a couple of minutes of silence, he said, "I'm sorry. I thought I could act normal, but I guess I can't." He glanced at her. "Or you're more perceptive than most."

"I'm sure I'm just amazing," she said, hoping to lighten his mood a little. "Lucky you to have me around. What happened?"

He clutched the steering wheel more tightly, then

exhaled. "One of my kids. Joey. He died last night. We knew it was coming. I tried everything I could think of. For a while it seemed like we were winning, but in the last couple of weeks…"

She had no idea what he was feeling. Death was as much a part of Josh's work as sweat was of hers. She couldn't begin to imagine what he must go through with each patient, knowing there was a chance that a child could die. But without his willingness to try, those lives would be lost for sure.

"He went downhill fast," he continued, slowly. "Faster than we thought. His body started shutting down late yesterday afternoon. He was gone by midnight."

"I'm sorry," she whispered. "It must hurt every time."

"It does. I nearly canceled getting the dog, but Alicia is really excited and she's still with us. Life has to go on, right?"

"You get involved," she said. "You have to mourn."

"I don't always have time. Every life is a battle. Me against the cancer. Sometimes I beat the bastard. Sometimes I don't. Even when the end is expected, it's still a shock. I was with Joey last night, along with his folks. I never know if staying is a good idea. If I help or make things worse."

"I'm sure his parents appreciate knowing how much you care. I would."

"Maybe. I know what they're going through. There's always hope—right to the end. That the hand of God is going to reach down and touch your loved one. That this time, there'll be a miracle."

He wasn't talking about the child anymore, she thought. "Was it like that with Stacey?" she asked softly.

"A little," he admitted. "By the time we knew the cancer was back, it was everywhere. Or maybe she knew earlier. I was never sure about that. She didn't want me to worry. We both knew once it returned, there wasn't going to be much for us to do. I kept on top of the research, but progress isn't made everywhere. When she got the diagnosis, she had less than six weeks to live."

Crissy hadn't known that. "I'm sorry," she said, wondering how anyone could survive the loss.

"She'd always known the cancer could come back," he continued. "In her heart, I think she believed it was just a matter of time. She lived her life knowing her years were limited. In the end, she made things as easy for me as she could. Isn't that crazy? She was the one dying and she wanted to make it okay for me."

There was too much emotion in his voice, Crissy thought, feeling as if he would later regret sharing so much. There was also a need to protect herself from this information. It would haunt her later. She had a feeling she would always be able to hear his voice, so filled with love and pain as he talked about the woman he had loved and married.

"But you go on," he said quietly. "You go on and while you never forget, eventually there's color in the world. You might not want there to be, but there is. Sometimes I tell that to the parents of my kids who die. Especially if they have other children at home."

His kids. She hadn't noticed that before. He called

them *his* kids. Because he was that closely connected? Or for another reason?

"It's like losing her all over again, isn't it?" she asked. "When you lose one of the children. You're re-living Stacey's death."

He looked at her. "Sometimes. How did you know?"

"It's not a big leap. You fight the same disease that killed your wife. You work with children who are innocent and far too young to die. Was Stacey all that different?"

He returned his attention to the road. "I'm sorry. I shouldn't be talking about this."

She didn't know if she agreed or not. It was difficult to have the conversation but ignoring these truths didn't make them go away.

"I know you were married before, Josh. I know you loved your wife very much. She is a part of who you are and she always will be."

Crissy knew all that in her head, although she'd yet to come to terms with the information in her heart. It wasn't that she wanted Josh *not* to have loved Stacey, it's that she wanted him to be able to move on. The jury was still out on that one.

"I shouldn't have brought you along today," he said.

That hurt, but she did her best not to react. "Because you'd rather be alone?"

"No. Because you didn't sign up for my problems. I'm sorry. I'm glad you're here, but it can't be much fun for you. Want me to take you back?"

The pain faded. "I'm happy to be here. Consider me your distraction for the day. Until we get the puppy.

Then you'll have a four-footed one to keep you from going to the dark place."

He reached across and took her hand in his. As his fingers laced with hers she wondered if she was making a mistake. Had she somehow become one of those women who fell for men they could never have? Or was she giving the man she cared about enough space to open his heart again?

Alicia was a pretty redhead with big green eyes and freckles. She practically trembled with excitement as Josh held out the squirming collie puppy.

"Her name is Sashay," he said with a grin. "She's pretty smart, so you're going to have to be a responsible pet owner. Are you ready to do that?"

Alicia nodded solemnly. She sat cross-legged on her family room floor, with her parents on the sofa, right behind her. Crissy stayed out of the inner circle, content to watch but not intrude on this surprisingly intimate moment.

There was a connection between Josh and the little girl, a bond she would guess had been forged by a battle against death.

Josh carefully handed over the puppy. Sashay sniffed Alicia, then swiped at her face with a long, pink tongue. Alicia giggled with delight and hugged the puppy close.

"I love her," the girl whispered. "I love her nearly as much as I love you, Dr. Josh."

"I'm glad," he said. "I brought my camera, so I want to take pictures."

But pictures had to wait for a while as Sashay met her new family. Crissy laughed as the puppy explored the family room and tumbled around with Alicia. When the two of them went out for a potty break, Josh and Alicia's father went along with them while Crissy followed Alicia's mother into the kitchen to make coffee.

"I'm not sure I'm ready for this," Jayne said, but she sounded happy. "A puppy is a lot of work."

"I think Alicia is going to be happy to help."

"I know she is. She's very responsible and empathetic. That happens to a lot of kids in her position. Being that sick and spending weeks in a hospital causes children to grow up quickly."

Jayne walked to the window over the sink and stared out into the backyard. Sashay and Alicia were running around the yard.

"She's so healthy now," Jayne said, her voice thick with emotion. "Look at how she runs."

"She's a beautiful girl," Crissy told her. "I would never guess she'd ever been sick."

"I know. Isn't that amazing. I give thanks every day. Do you have children?"

Crissy thought briefly of Brandon and knew she couldn't rightfully claim him as her own. "No."

"When you do, you'll understand. I was terrified when she was diagnosed. Things only got worse as doctor after doctor said there was nothing they could do. Treatments for her kind of cancer were too difficult for children. The risks were too high. No one would help. Then we met Dr. Josh. He said sometimes there's a miracle. With Alicia, there was."

Jayne busied herself with putting cookies on a plate. She sniffed, then looked up. "We were so afraid. Even after all this time, I remember the terror. But he was with us. When we started the treatments, when she only got sicker. He was right there. I can't remember how many nights I spent at the hospital. I would wake up in the bed next to hers and Dr. Josh would be sitting beside her, holding her hand, whispering that she was going to get better and that she had to hang on. He poured his whole heart and soul into making her well and it worked. We owe him everything."

"I'm sure Josh doesn't see it that way," Crissy said, not completely surprised to hear about his involvement with the family.

"He doesn't," Jayne told her. "He's like that for all his patients. He's an incredible man, but then you probably know that."

"I do."

Crissy was very clear on Josh's good points. But were they also his flaws? Did he give so much to his kids that he had nothing left for anyone else? Was he hiding behind his work because it was easier than facing a life of his own?

The questions made her feel guilty—like she was actively looking for trouble. Without his commitment, Alicia might not be alive. Did she, Crissy, wish things were any different?

She knew the answer to that, but she was still confused about the situation. Did Josh know how to balance work and personal life? Did he want to? What, exactly, was he looking for from her? What did she want from him? How were either of them going to handle their relationship if she found out she was pregnant?

The next couple of days were difficult for Crissy. She didn't see Josh and wasn't sure if he was as busy as he claimed or if he was avoiding her after exposing too much of himself. She was currently voting for the busy being real, but wasn't sure if her luck was that good.

Because she didn't have enough on her worry list, she went out and bought two different pregnancy kits. Only a couple more days until she would know if she was pregnant or not. Sometimes she was convinced she was playing a head game with herself and other times she was positive she was "with child" as her grandmother used to say.

In a desperate attempt to distract herself, she decided to clean the bathrooms in her house. It was a job she loathed. Even laundry was better than scrubbing toilets and the shower. She collected all the equipment and cleaning products she would need, then pulled on her rubber gloves. But before she could get started, the phone rang.

Her brain went immediately into "Josh or not-Josh" mode. She glanced at the clock and figured it was unlikely that he would be calling at eight-fifteen in the evening.

"Hello?"

"Crissy? Thank God. It's Abbey. I'm sorry to bother you, but I have no one else."

Abbey sounded breathless and frantic. Crissy ripped off her gloves, then began searching for shoes.

"You're not bothering me. What happened? How can I help?"

"It's Hope. She has asthma. She's having a horrible attack. I've called nine-one-one and they'll be here any second. I know they're going to take her to the hospital and I have to go with her. Pete's at the station, my neighbors are gone, I can't find Josh. I can't leave the other two kids alone."

"Give me your cell number," Crissy said, then wrote it down. "Go now. Right now. Tell Brandon to lock the door behind you and that I'll be there in fifteen minutes. He can be alone for that long, can't he?"

"What? Yes. Emma's already in bed. I don't know how to thank you."

"Don't. Just go."

Crissy drove as carefully as she could. The last thing any of them needed was for her to get in an accident. She arrived at Abbey's house seventeen minutes after hanging up and saw the paramedics had arrived before her.

There was a fire truck parked in front of the house and a paramedic van in the driveway. Flashing red lights cut through the night.

Crissy found a spot a couple of houses away, then hurried to the front door. It was open and she stepped inside.

Hope lay on a gurney, with an oxygen mask on her face. Abbey bent over her, soothing her. Two paramedics prepared to transport her.

Crissy glanced around and saw Brandon and Emma

huddled together by the stairs. She hurried over and crouched in front of them.

"Hey, guys. This is scary, huh?"

They both nodded.

She touched Emma's arm. "Do you remember who I am, honey?"

Emma stared at her. "Mommy's friend. Crissy."

"That's right. I'm going to stay with you tonight." She had no idea how long she was going to be there, so didn't bother trying to state a time. "Your mom will go the hospital with Hope."

Brandon put his arm around his sister. "She's been sick before. It's scary, but she gets better."

Emma's eyes were huge. "Can I go with Mommy?"

"I know you want to," Crissy said. "But it's late and she'll be busy helping Hope. The three of us will spend the night together. Like a sleepover. How's that?"

Emma didn't look convinced. Abbey hurried over.

"I can't thank you enough," she said.

"Don't worry about it. I'm glad I was around to help."

Abbey kissed her kids. "Be good for Crissy. I don't know if we'll be back tonight or in the morning. Daddy will come home when he can, but it shouldn't be later than seven. Okay?"

They nodded.

Abbey smiled. "Good. We're all going to be fine and that's what matters. Now let me talk to Crissy for a minute, okay?" She pulled Crissy into the hallway.

"Pete's at a fire," she said in a low voice. "He'll leave the station as soon as he gets my message, but I don't know how long he'll be. He'll come home and relieve you."

Crissy shook her head. "Let him go to the hospital to check on Hope first. The kids and I will be okay."

"Are you sure? That would be great if he could be with me. I could use the support."

"Absolutely."

"Thank you. Josh will probably come by when he gets my message. If you could stand to let the kids hang out with you on the family room sofa, that would be best. Eventually they'll fall asleep. But I don't want to make them go back to their rooms. They get scared when stuff like this happens."

"Of course they do." Crissy was terrified and she was a grown-up.

"We're ready," one of the paramedics told Abbey.

She nodded, kissed her kids and went out with Hope. In a matter of seconds, the sound of the siren filled the house and then that, too, was gone.

Crissy turned back to Brandon and Emma. They both looked small and young, standing together, looking expectantly at her as if waiting for her to make things right.

"I think a movie is in order," she said. "Something funny." And distracting, she thought. They all needed that. "Brandon, why don't you go pick out three movies and we'll choose between them. Oh, and maybe grab some blankets so we can cuddle up properly. Emma, let's go in the kitchen. You can show me where everything is so we can have a snack. Does your mom ever make hot chocolate?"

The girl looked at her with big, frightened eyes. For a second Crissy thought she might burst into tears. Then Emma sniffed, took her hand and led the way into the kitchen.

"There's chocolate and marshmallows," she said, her voice a little thick. "The big ones. Can I have two?"

"Sure. I think we'll all have two marshmallows with our hot chocolate."

Thirty minutes later they were curled up together on the sofa watching a cartoon movie that had both kids laughing. The hot chocolate had been a big hit. Even Crissy had appreciated the familiar and comforting flavor.

She sat in the middle of the large sectional sofa, with a child on each side of her. Emma kept nodding off. Finally she put her head down on the pillow that Brandon had brought from her room and went to sleep.

Crissy glanced at Brandon, who seemed completely awake.

"There's a little left," she said, motioning to his mug. "I could heat it up for you."

"Okay."

She stood then made sure Emma was tucked in and comfortable before heading to the kitchen. Both kids had been great, she thought, grateful no one had given in to hysterics.

She wondered how long it would be before they heard anything from the hospital, then sent up a prayer that little Hope would be all right.

As she picked up the small pot to put it back on the stove, she heard a noise and turned. Brandon stood just inside the kitchen. He looked troubled and scared and a lot of other emotions she couldn't define.

"Brandon? What's wrong?" she asked as she put down the pot and crossed to him. She crouched in front of him and smiled. "Scared about Hope?"

He shrugged. "Yeah, but…" He cleared his throat and stared into her eyes. "Are you my mom?"

Chapter Eight

Crissy swallowed hard. She felt another wave of panic, but this one had nothing to do with Hope's asthma.

What was she supposed to say? How could she handle this? She wasn't prepared. She didn't have the answers to tell herself, let alone a twelve-year-old boy. It was crazy.

She'd thought that eventually she'd want to have this conversation with Brandon, but not now. Not unexpectedly, when they were alone and there was no one to guide her through this.

He shoved his hands into his jeans pockets and looked away. "I heard my mom and dad talking about you. About how you were getting involved in my life, which is what they always wanted. How it was good for me to know you." He shrugged.

"Oh, Brandon," she whispered, not sure if she should pull him close and hug him or let him stand alone.

She didn't know anything about him or how to make things better for him. Which was only her own fault. Why hadn't she been willing to be a part of her son's life? Why hadn't she done this years ago?

Her throat tightened and her eyes burned. She wasn't sure if the tears she held back were for him or herself. Maybe both.

"I didn't want to say anything to them," he mumbled. "But I wondered."

Not knowing what else to do, she put her arm around his shoulders. "How long have you known this?" she asked.

"A couple of days."

"That's a pretty big burden to carry. It must have been hard. Then with Hope getting sick…you've had a rough week."

"I can handle it."

He sounded tough, but he was only twelve.

There was no one to help her with this situation. She would have to deal with it as best she could.

"Come on," she said as she stood and led the way to the kitchen table. "Let's talk."

He followed her and took a seat. She went to the stove where she heated the last of the hot chocolate, poured it into a mug, added two marshmallows, then set it in front of him. She took the seat across from his.

"I don't know where to start," she admitted. "I guess the big announcement first makes the most sense. Yes, I'm your birth mother."

He'd been staring at his mug, but now he looked at her. "For sure?"

She smiled. "Yes. For sure." Her smile faded. "I didn't plan this conversation. I don't know what to tell you or what you want to know. Would it be easier for you to ask questions or do you want me to talk?"

He swallowed, then looked at her. "You were young, right?"

Oh God. The pain of being rejected by the woman who gave birth to you. It *had* to be what he was thinking.

"I was seventeen," she said, aching for him and not sure how to make it all better. "Five years older than you are now."

"Four and a half. I'll be thirteen this summer."

"Right." At his age, getting older was important, she reminded herself. "So I was four and a half years older than you are now. I was supposed to go to college and suddenly I was in high school and pregnant. I didn't know what to do."

"Were your parents mad?"

"Not mad so much as disappointed. But they wanted to be supportive, which was great. I didn't think I was ready to be a mom, so we talked about adopting. But that was hard, too. I mean I wanted to find the right people. The perfect parents. I didn't know if I could." She smiled. "Then I met Pete and Abbey."

He seemed to relax a little. "You liked them?"

"From the second I saw them. They were so in love. Kind of like they are now."

He wrinkled his nose. "They're always kissing. It's gross."

"You'll like it more as you get older. I liked everything about them. They were so excited at the thought of you. They had plans for your room and adopting other brothers and sisters for you. They talked about family vacations and how they wanted you to grow up. I knew they were the ones from the moment we met."

He brightened a little. "That's cool."

"It was. Abbey was there with me when you were born. She held you right away and I knew by the look on her face how much she loved you."

He grinned and looked uncomfortable at the same time.

"One of things I really liked about them was how they were so open about the adoption," she continued. "They wanted you to know from the beginning. Abbey sent pictures and letters, telling me how you were, so I could watch you grow up."

"But you didn't come see me."

She knew she had to tread carefully here. She wasn't interested in protecting herself as much as she wanted to make this as easy for Brandon as possible.

"I didn't know how to be involved without everything being confusing," she admitted. "Abbey is one of those women who knows exactly how to be a mom. I'm not. One of the reasons I picked adoption was that I was terrified of doing everything wrong. It was part of being young. So I thought letting you grow up feeling safe and secure was the best thing."

She would tell him more later—when he was older and could understand about regrets and second-guessing.

"But lately I've had this feeling that it was time," she said. "I contacted your parents and they agreed that we should get to know each other. If everything went well, we would figure out a way to tell you who I was. I guess we don't have to have that conversation now."

One corner of his mouth turned up. "I guess not."

"I'm sorry you overheard that conversation. It must have been really hard to learn that and not be able to talk about it."

He shrugged. "I didn't know what to tell my mom. I didn't know what she was thinking or how mad she'd be. Not that she gets mad at stuff like that. I thought a lot about it. It's weird, you know? The parent stuff. With my friends, I see how someone looks like his dad or turns his head like his brother. I never had that. But with you…"

"Same eyes, same smile."

"I'm good at sports," he said eagerly. "You're good at sports, too."

"So's your dad," she said without thinking.

Brandon's expression changed to one of hopeful longing. "You mean my birth dad?"

Crissy wasn't sure if that was the term for it, but it worked. It was classier than "the guy who got her pregnant and didn't want to marry her." Not that she'd been interested in getting married, either, but still.

"Yes, your birth dad. Marty. He played football in high school. You look a lot like him. He was funny and smart. He went to West Point. Do you know what that—"

Brandon cut her off with an impatient eye roll. "Yes, I know. It's the Army college for officers. One of my friend's sisters goes there. They let girls in now."

Crissy couldn't tell if he was impressed or revolted by the thought.

"I've lost touch with him," she said. "I could try to find him, if you'd like."

Brandon shrugged. "Maybe later."

Right. Because one new birth parent was probably enough.

"You're also a lot like my dad and my brother," she said. "Your build."

His eyes widened. "You have a brother?"

"And a sister. My parents are still alive, so I'm thinking you have a whole lot more family out there."

"Do they know about me?"

"Absolutely. They know I've been meeting you and they're hoping they can meet you, too." Her entire family was threatening a visit in the not too distant future. "More grandparents is a pretty cool thing. Plus, I have nieces and nephews, which means you have cousins. You're the oldest."

Crissy wanted to say more, like that they would all get together at some point, but she didn't want to over-commit. Not when Brandon was just learning about her and her family and she didn't know how everything was going to play out.

She knew her parents would be thrilled to finally meet him.

"Brandon," she said slowly. "What happened all those years ago was about me. I was young and scared and I didn't know what to do. Pete and Abbey were so great that I knew they deserved you. I wanted what was best for you."

And easiest for her, she thought with a flash of guilt.

Yet even as she started to beat herself up, she wondered if she really could have done a better job raising him. She'd been a kid with no job, no education. She had many great qualities, but she wasn't a born mother, like Abbey. Could she truly say that keeping Brandon would have been better for him?

Before he could say anything, there was a knock on the front door. Crissy and Brandon walked toward it, then Brandon broke into a run and jerked open the front door.

"Uncle Josh," he said, flinging himself at the man. "You came. Mom tried to call you before, but you didn't answer."

"I'm sorry," he said, pulling Brandon close. "My battery went out on my pager. I didn't realize it until I figured out it had been quiet for too long."

He looked at her over Brandon's head. "Is everything all right?"

All the strength drained out of her. She, too, wanted to be in his capable arms and have him hold her close. She wanted to know that he would take care of her and whatever problems she had.

"Hope got sick," Brandon said. "Her asthma was really bad and she couldn't breathe. Mom had to call nine-one-one. Dad's at a fire and you didn't answer your pager and the neighbors are all gone, so she called Crissy. Emma was real scared when the ambulance arrived. She's asleep now. Crissy came and we watched a movie and made hot chocolate."

"Sounds like things here are under control," Josh said as he watched her. "You okay?"

She wasn't sure, but she didn't want to say that in front of Brandon. So she nodded.

"Good." Josh released his nephew and smiled at him. "I think PJs are in order."

"Mom said we could sleep on the sofa in the family room. You know, together, so Emma doesn't get scared."

"Good idea. Go get changed and we'll all crash on the sofa. How does that sound?"

"Great."

Brandon ran down the hall.

When they were alone, Josh crossed to her and put his hands on her shoulders. "What's wrong? You look upset. Did the Hope thing freak you out?"

"It was horrible, but no. Abbey handled all that." She glanced around to make sure Brandon hadn't returned, then lowered her voice. "He knows who I am. When Emma fell asleep, he asked me if I was his birth mother. I didn't know what to say. He overheard Pete and Abbey talking a couple of days ago. I felt so horrible that he'd been carrying that around inside."

Josh swore softly. "I'm with you on that. Poor kid. What did you tell him?"

"The truth. That I was. We've been talking about it, but I don't know if I said too much or not enough. I don't know if he's all right or more confused. What if he hates me?"

Josh leaned in and kissed her. "He doesn't hate you. He totally respects how you play football and for a twelve-year-old boy, that's close to worship."

She wanted that to be true, although at this point, just tolerating her seemed like a win.

"I feel so bad that he had to go through that alone," she said. "What if I made things worse?"

"You didn't," Josh said firmly. "Want me to talk to him and confirm my theory?"

"That would be great."

Josh saw the worry in Crissy's eyes and heard the concern in her voice. He liked that she'd connected so much with Brandon. Now that the kid knew the truth, there was no going back. Having Crissy care so much would make things easier for Brandon.

"Be right back," he said and followed his nephew down that hall. A quick glance at his watch told him it was after ten. In another hour he would call the hospital and check on Hope's condition.

He walked into Brandon's room. "You ready for some serious relaxation?"

"Uh-huh."

Josh sat on the boy's bed and patted the spot next to him. "Have a seat."

Brandon eyed him warily. "What? Oh." His expression cleared. "Crissy told you what I said."

"She did and I want to make sure you're handling it all right. Talk about a lot of information."

Brandon sank onto the bed. "It wasn't so bad. I knew I was adopted and I guess I always sort of figured I had a mother out there. Sometimes I thought she might be dead. I didn't spend a lot of time wondering, you know?"

He didn't, but he could imagine. "Crissy's pretty cool."

Brandon shot him a grin. "For a girl."

"Don't let her hear you say that."

"I know. Man, she's really sensitive about the girl thing. But I like her, so it's okay."

Josh wasn't sure how much to say or what questions to ask. The only thing he knew for sure was to make sure Brandon understood he was loved and wanted. "She was pretty young when she got pregnant."

"That's what she said. In high school. That's real young to have a baby. It's better to wait until you're older and married." He grimaced. "I don't know if I want to get married."

Josh held in a chuckle. "You don't have to decide tonight. The point is her decision to give you up for adoption was about where she was. It wasn't about you."

"She told me that, too. Jeez. I know Mom and Dad love me, okay? I'm not going to start acting up because I don't feel special."

Josh grabbed him and wrestled him onto his back, then tickled his ribs. "You think you're so smart. You think you know everything."

"I am smart," Brandon gasped as he laughed and squirmed. "Okay, okay. I give."

Josh released him. "They wanted you. From the second they met Crissy, they wanted you. I was still in medical school. I remember Pete meeting me outside one of my classrooms at lunch. He'd said it was really important." Josh grinned as he remembered his brother's excitement. "He went on and on about the pregnant high-school girl he and Abbey had met the night before. How great she was and how much she wanted the best for her baby. Pete said he knew that baby, her baby, was the one. That he or she was going to be their firstborn. That was you, kid."

"Yeah?" Brandon straightened and squared his shoulders. "I am amazing."

Josh laughed. "Yes, you are. A little self-absorbed, but I can tickle that out of you."

Brandon scooted out of range.

"They love you," Josh said.

"I *know* that."

"We're all going to be really boring and keep repeating that. Crissy being your birth mother doesn't change who you are or where you belong."

Brandon picked at the L.A. Dodger comforter. "She's got family. Parents. A brother and sister. They have kids. So they're kind of related to me, too." He looked up, his expression stricken. "Is that okay?"

"Of course. You're allowed to have blood relatives."

"I know, but I don't want Mom or Dad to think they matter less, you know? Or you. I mean I have another uncle now, but he'll never be like you."

Josh grabbed Brandon and pulled him close. "You get to love as many people as you want. It's better that way. More family is a good thing and your folks will be cool with that."

"I'd never hurt them."

"They know that. So you'll get to know Crissy and meet the rest of your family. They'll become a part of you, but this will always be your home."

The boy relaxed. "Promise?"

"Absolutely."

Later, when Brandon had fallen asleep on the sectional sofa, Josh joined Crissy in the kitchen.

"And?" she asked. "Is it all right? Did I damage him permanently or can it be repaired?"

She looked worried and scared and more beautiful than he'd ever seen her. He crossed to where she stood by the cabinets, put his hands on her waist and then leaned in and kissed her.

She tasted of chocolate and temptation. Even though their lips barely touched and their bodies didn't, wanting exploded inside of him. He ignored it, knowing this wasn't the time or the place. But later?

"He's fine. Better than fine," he said. "He's good. He understands what you told him, he doesn't blame you for giving him up. His biggest worry is that he's excited to meet the rest of your family and he doesn't want that to hurt Pete or Abbey."

Relief relaxed her features. "You sure? You're not just saying that to make me feel better?"

"I swear, he's doing great." He recapped his conversation with Brandon. "As he pointed out, it helped that he knew he was adopted. So he's always wondered about his birth mother. Overhearing what he heard only filled in the pieces for him. You've made the first step and it's a good one."

She exhaled slowly. "That's a relief. I was stunned when he flat out asked if I was his birth mother. I couldn't believe we were alone and there was no one to guide me through the conversation. I had to rely on instinct."

"Your instincts are working just fine," he said as he touched her face.

"Good to know. I want to talk to Abbey about all this. She's going to get even more questions from him, I'm sure. She'll be okay with this, right? She won't hate me?"

"She won't hate you."

"She's such a good person. I really respect her. And admire her. I want to be a part of Brandon's life, but not as his mom. Abbey will always be that. She should be. But I could be someone else."

"Be you," he said, then kissed her again.

The wanting rose again. This time it was more insistent and accompanied by a physical manifestation. Rather than give in, he led her to the table where he was careful to sit far enough away that she was out of touching distance.

"What a night." She leaned back in her chair. "What's going on with Hope, do you think? Is she going to be all right?"

"I'm not a specialist, but I would guess she'll do fine. She has the kind of asthma most kids outgrow. It's scary but not always life-threatening."

She smiled. "You're a good guy to have around. I'm sure Pete and Abbey appreciate how great you are with the kids."

"It's takes a village," he teased, watching the way her mouth moved when she smiled.

"In my case, it would take more of a town. I'm not the maternal type. But you seem to have the instinct." She studied him. "I've seen you with Abbey's kids, and with Alicia a couple of days ago. You're terrific with kids. You know what to say and they adore you. So why don't you have any of your own? Did you hold off because of Stacey's illness?"

An innocent question, he thought, his good mood fading. A reasonable one, under the circumstances. But still, his insides knotted.

"I never wanted children," he told her. "My work keeps me busy and I'm around kids all day so I've never felt the loss. Stacey couldn't have kids, so that worked out. It was just the two of us. We talked about adopting, but our hearts weren't in it. Once she got sick, we both realized we'd made the right decision."

Josh kept talking, but Crissy wasn't listening. Her brain was stuck on his casual "I never wanted children."

It wasn't possible. She refused to believe it. How could he not want kids? He was great with them. They adored him. He had instincts she could only dream about. He was born to be a father. He worked with children every day. So why didn't he want any of his own?

She didn't have any answers, which was pretty scary. What if she *was* pregnant? Did that mean Josh wouldn't want to be a part of his child's life? Just as important, what about her relationship with him? She'd thought he was someone she could genuinely care about. She thought he could matter.

But however much she might be lacking the "mom" gene, she'd always seen herself having a family of her own someday. She couldn't be with a man who wasn't willing to share that.

The phone rang, breaking through her whirlwind of thoughts. Josh grabbed it.

"Hello?"

He listened for a minute, then smiled. "Good. I'm

glad she's okay. I'll tell Crissy and the kids. Yes. Sure. Okay. See you when you get here."

He hung up. "Hope's fine. She and Abbey will stay the night at the hospital, just to be sure, then they'll be home in the morning."

"That's a relief," Crissy said.

"She's leaving a message for Pete, telling him to go ahead and finish out his shift. I'm going to stay the night here. I've done it before. I have clothes in the guest room. You can head home if you want."

Home? Right. She could go home.

She stood and wondered what she was supposed to say now. Judging from how Josh kept talking it was obvious he didn't know he'd upset her, which was probably a good thing. She had no idea what she could say to him.

Her first reaction was to tell him he didn't know what he was talking about. Of course he wanted children. But did she really know him? Making love with a man didn't entitle her to the secrets of his soul. He could very well be telling the truth. She could be caught up in a big fat case of wishful thinking.

"I should go," she said as she rose. "I have a busy day tomorrow."

He stood and pulled her close. "You didn't have to come over and take care of things like you did."

"It was a crisis. I wasn't going to refuse."

"I like that about you."

She gazed up into his eyes and wondered if it was too late not to care about him. "You need higher standards."

"My standards are plenty high. You meet all of them."

She forced herself to smile, then kiss him before leaving.

As she walked to the car, she knew that he was wrong about her. She didn't meet all his standards. She wanted children and the loud, happy mess of a life that came with them. She might not have been ready before, when she'd gotten pregnant with Brandon, but she was now.

It had taken her the past twelve years to figure out she could forgive herself for making the decision she had and finally allow herself to be happy. She knew what she wanted. If Josh didn't want the same things she did—he wasn't right for her.

Simple enough to say, she thought sadly as she drove into the night. But walking away wasn't going to be easy. He was the best man she'd ever met. How was she supposed to find someone better?

Two mornings later Crissy stared at the neat row of plastic sticks. Some came with pluses, others had writing, but all the messages were exactly the same.

She was pregnant.

Chapter Nine

Saturday morning Crissy drove over to join Rachel for Noelle's "Baby Watch." Noelle was close enough to popping that no one wanted her to be by herself. Dev had out-of-town clients he had to deal with so Rachel and Crissy had volunteered to be on duty.

When she'd agreed to help out, she'd thought only of being with her friend. Now as she curled up on the sofa in the well-decorated, bright family room, she thought about how much these women had come to mean to her.

They'd only known each other a little over two years, but in that time, they'd become so close. They'd gone through more than different knitting classes—they'd seen each other's lives change for the better. She couldn't imagine not having them to lean on.

Crissy watched as Noelle shifted in the chair.

"I can't get comfortable," she complained. "I was willing to be brave about it for a while, but now I'm just plain cranky. Do I have to be so huge? I'm not giving birth to a pod of whales. It should be just one seven or eight pound baby."

"That's a lot of baby," Rachel said, sounding impressed.

"I'm still caught up on her knowing that whales traveled in pods," Crissy teased. "Someone's been watching *Animal Planet.*"

Noelle sighed. "I'm serious. I want the baby out now. I don't care how."

Crissy looked at Rachel. "She does have that great knife set in the kitchen."

Rachel rubbed the sofa fabric. "The blood would stain."

"That's a problem."

Noelle glared at her. "Take me seriously!"

Crissy crossed to the ottoman in front of her chair and grabbed one of her hands. "I know you're uncomfortable, but it's only for a few more days. Hang on. It's going to be worth it. You'll see."

Noelle's eyes filled with tears. "I know. I just want to see her so much. My back hurts, I'm swollen up like a water balloon. I look hideous. Dev is never going to be able to forget how hideous I look and he won't want to have sex with me again."

Crissy's pain during her first pregnancy had been about missing the prom. She hadn't had to think in terms of babies or marriages. Things were different when one was a grown-up.

"Now you're scaring me," Rachel said with a whimper in her voice. "I've changed my mind about being pregnant."

"Don't do that," Noelle told her. "It's wonderful. Really. I'm just having a bad day. Let's change the subject to something fun. Like the wedding. How are plans coming?"

"Slowly," Rachel said. "We haven't set a date yet, but it will definitely be after the baby's born. I want to be skinny in my dress."

Crissy returned to the sofa. "You'll be a beautiful bride."

"I'll do my best. I keep waiting for Carter's family to get upset because I'm pregnant first and married later, but everyone has been great. After I lost my family all those years ago, I never thought I'd have that again. But now I do. He gave me a family."

Her voice cracked as she spoke, then she wiped away tears. Noelle looked a little misty.

"Am I the only one still sane?" Crissy asked, worried that they were all about to start sobbing in unison, or worse, break out in song. "Let's talk about something that doesn't involve emotions. Wallpaper, maybe. Or some great barbecue ideas for the summer."

Rachel wiped her eyes. "Sorry. You're right. It must be really hard for you to deal with us. The whole pregnancy thing. I guess it's like being the only sober person at a big party. You've been so there for us. We're going to have to figure out a way to pay you back."

Crissy opened her mouth, then closed it. To be honest, she'd been living in the happy land of denial for the past couple of days. The pregnancy tests had told her a truth she didn't want to admit, so she'd ignored it. With the exception of giving up wine—hardly difficult as she rarely drank—and being sure she took her vitamins every day, she hadn't changed anything about her life.

But like it or not, in about eight months, she was going to have a baby.

She still wasn't sure how she felt about that. Part of her was practically giddy at the thought. A baby. She could handle a child now. She was more mature, more financially settled. She had a support system in place.

Part of her thought she was crazy. A baby? She didn't know the first thing about being a mother. Her idea of domestic was to buy lettuce and salad dressing separately, instead of together in one of those premade salad bags. Had she thought to get Noelle a wonderfully practical present for the shower? A stroller or high chair or even diaper service? Not her. She'd gone with frilly dresses the baby would never wear.

There was also the complication of Josh, but she didn't want to think about that because if she did, she would panic and that wouldn't be pretty.

"Crissy?"

She looked up and saw both Noelle and Rachel staring at her.

"What's wrong?" Noelle asked.

"Nothing. I'm fine. Great even. Perfect."

Rachel frowned. "You don't look fine. You're not your normal bouncy self. What's going on? Did something happen with Brandon?"

"Or with Josh?" Noelle asked.

"I…"

Something had happened with both of them. Something big.

"I…"

"You're keeping secrets," Rachel said, sounding disappointed. "Are you mad at us? Have we been too self-absorbed with our pregnancies? Do you hate us?"

Noelle instantly teared up. "Oh God. You think we're too domestic. You're so sophisticated. You have a successful business and you're beautiful. I'm just some kid who got knocked up, right? You don't want to be friends with me anymore. You think I'm stupid."

Now the tears were flowing freely. Rachel looked as if she was seconds from giving in to emotion, as well. Crissy wanted to pound her head against the wall.

"Stop," she said. "Just stop. I love you guys. I want to be friends, in fact I insist on it. I need you both. I'm going to need you a whole lot more in the next few months."

They both stared at her. "What happened?" Rachel asked.

"A lot. I didn't say anything because I've been sort of ignoring it myself. I think I've reached my crisis limit for this week." She drew in a breath. It was probably better to start small and build up to the big announcement.

"Brandon knows I'm his birth mother."

That stopped the tears.

Noelle wiped her face. "What happened?"

Crissy explained about Hope's asthma attack and how she, Crissy, had gone over to help out.

"He just asked," she said, remembering how she'd felt at that moment. "I honestly didn't know what to say, how to explain. I didn't want to hurt him or make him feel bad. I sort of let him lead the conversation. Later, when I talked to Abbey, she said everything had gone great and that Brandon was doing well. I hope she's right."

Rachel grinned at her. "So he knows you're his mother."

"Birth mother. And yes, there's a difference. Abbey's his mom. She's been the one raising him for nearly thirteen years. I'm just…the vessel."

"You're more than that," Noelle told her. "Besides, you want to be involved, don't you? You want to be in his life."

Crissy smiled. "I do. It's so strange. I avoided thinking about him for years, but now that I've met him and I've seen our connection, I want more. I want to be a part of his world."

"Regrets?" Rachel asked.

"Some. In my crazy moments, I wonder what it would have been like. But the rest of the time I know I made the right choice."

"So you'll be there for him, giving him advice." Noelle shifted in her chair. "You'll have the best of it. You get to be the cool adult in his life."

"I'd like that."

"So this is good," Rachel said. "You should be happy."

"I am, about that. But there's more." Crissy drew in a breath. How to explain the complications of Josh. "I, um… There are complications other than Brandon."

"I thought you liked Josh," Noelle said. "Don't you?"

"I do. A lot. He's a great guy. If I were to make a list

of everything I want, he would hit all the high points. On the surface, he's practically perfect, but underneath…not so much."

"Meaning?" Rachel asked.

"He's still in love with Stacey."

"You don't know that," Noelle said firmly. "He'll always have feelings for her. He'd be a jerk if he didn't. But that's not the same as being in love."

"I know the difference and I have a feeling he's falling on the 'in love' side of things. He hasn't been with anyone but me since she died. That was four years ago. Don't you think that's taking mourning just a little too far?"

Rachel and Noelle exchanged a look that told Crissy the two of them had been talking about her situation.

"But he's with you now," Noelle said. "That has to mean something."

"It does…"

"But?" Rachel asked.

"But I'm confused about a few things. What he does, helping those sick kids. It takes a lot out of him. He takes on the cases no one else will. It's admirable. But does knowing any one of them could die mean he gets to hold back?"

She covered her face with her hands, then straightened and looked at her friends. "Okay, here's my terrible thought for the day. Stacey had a kind of cancer that was likely to return. Odds were, when it did, it would claim her life. He knew that and he still wanted to marry her. Which is admirable. But is it possible part of the reason he loved her was that she was safe? Did he marry her knowing he would lose her and did that mean he didn't have to give so much of himself? And am I a completely horrible person for thinking that?"

"No," Rachel said immediately. "You can think what you think. No one judges that."

"You're too hard on yourself." Noelle rubbed her belly. "I can see why you're worried, but it's possible you're reading too much into the situation. Maybe he married Stacey because he fell in love with her and a short life together was better than no time at all. I would do that with Dev in a heartbeat. There doesn't have to be a deep, dark, psychological reason for his actions."

There didn't have to be, but Crissy couldn't help wondering if there was. "My gut is warning me that this might be a guy who is emotionally unavailable. Do I need that kind of hassle in my life?"

"Are you willing to walk away?" Rachel asked.

Crissy shook her head. "It's too late for that. The thing is I spent so many years beating myself up about Brandon. I decided I'd done something wrong, so I continued to punish myself. I wouldn't get serious about anyone. I picked guys who could never understand me, losers who could never be my partner in life. It got so bad, I swore off dating forever. Then I met Josh and he's amazing. But have I come all this way and learned all these life lessons only to fall for a guy who's emotionally unavailable?"

"You're assuming the worst about him," Rachel said. "Maybe give him a chance to prove himself before you jump all over him."

"Oh, but that would make sense," Crissy teased. Then her humor faded. "He doesn't want children."

"What?" Noelle sounded outraged. "No. That can't be right. He works with kids. You said he was great with Abbey and Pete's kids."

"I know, but that's what he told me. He came by after I'd talked to Brandon and he seemed to know exactly what to say to both of us. So I asked him why he and Stacey hadn't had kids. He said she couldn't and he'd never wanted them."

"Okay, now I get it," Rachel said. "He probably never thought about having children. Then he fell madly in love with someone who couldn't have them so he convinced himself he didn't want them in the first place so he wouldn't hurt her feelings."

That's what Crissy wanted to believe, too. "That's the best case scenario. But how can I know if he did a mind shift for his late wife or if he really doesn't want children?"

"You have to find out which," Noelle said firmly. "Because you do want a family. I know you joke about the horrors of fluids in pregnancy and all that, but I know you, Crissy. You want a family."

Crissy nodded. "I do. I don't know how to find out the truth about Josh. I can't exactly ask him if he'll let me work up a psychological profile. So I'm left with some serious gray matter. In theory, the no-kids thing is a deal breaker."

"In theory?" Rachel looked at her. "You'd consider not having a family because of him?"

"Not exactly. There's another complication."

Noelle shook her head. "I've never understood why people watch soap operas, but I'm beginning to see the appeal. All the drama is very compelling. So what's the complication? You're attracted to Pete? Abbey's at-tracted to Josh? They want you to be a surrogate mother for them? Josh hates your cat?"

Despite everything, Crissy laughed. "It's not a matter of him liking King Edward, it's whether or not King Edward will like him."

"Of course," Rachel said. "We know who's in charge. So what is it?"

Crissy drew in a deep breath. "I'm pregnant."

Both women stared at her in disbelief—wide-eyed, mouths open. Rachel recovered first and flung herself at Crissy.

"You're going to have a baby? That's wonderful. I'm so happy for you. I can't believe we're all pregnant together? What are the odds of that? It's the knitting class. And to think you hate the yarn."

Crissy hugged her friend, appreciating the comfort and the support.

"I don't hate the yarn," she said. "It hates me."

Noelle sniffed. "I can't get up and come over. You guys have to come to me."

Both of them moved toward the chair where they huddled in a group hug. Finally everyone settled back in their seats.

"Are you happy?" Noelle asked. "It's got to be a shock."

"It is," Crissy admitted. "I've been ignoring the obvious—that thirteen years after it happened the first time, I'm once again dealing with an unplanned preg-nancy. Obviously I'm a slow learner in this area."

"But you're happy," Noelle said. "Aren't you?"

Crissy smiled slowly. "I'm very happy. A little surprised, but happy. I feel ready this time. I'm grown-up and I can do this. Sort of." She felt fear nibbling at the edges of her happiness. "Except I'm not very maternal. Do you think the baby will mind?"

"You'll do great," Rachel said. "If you get worried, just call one of us. By the time you have your baby, we'll be experts."

"Good point." Crissy relaxed a little. "I want this," she admitted. "I want all of it. The messy, fluid-filled baby stuff. I want to be there for every moment. I want to watch my child grow up while knowing my life will never be the same."

Her friends nodded as if they, too, felt that.

"But," Rachel said. "What about Josh?"

"There is that."

"Maybe you misunderstood him," Noelle said. "Maybe he was just talking about before. When it was with Stacey."

"Maybe." But Crissy was doubtful. "I have to tell him and I honestly don't know what he's going to say."

"He might surprise you in a good way," Rachel said. "Saying you don't want children is one thing, but being faced with a baby of his own is another. He might discover he wants to be a father. You said he gives everything to the sick children he works with. How could he give less to his own son or daughter?"

A good question. In theory, Crissy agreed with her, but in her gut, she wondered and worried.

"I won't know until we have the conversation," she said.

"Which will be when?" Noelle asked.

"I don't know. I'm going to put it off for a couple of weeks. Let the whole Brandon thing die down. If Josh and I could spend a little more time together, I might get him figured out. That would help. But I'm not waiting longer than that. I want to feel safe in the conversation but I don't want him thinking I was trying to keep the information from him. Talk about a balancing act…"

"You're up to it," Rachel told her. "It will be fine. You'll see."

"He'll come through in the end," Noelle said. "He's one of the good guys."

Crissy could only hope her friends were right.

Three days later Crissy knew she was acting like a total coward, which wasn't her style at all. She'd been lying low and avoiding Josh, which wasn't helping her "get to know him better" plan.

He'd called and they'd talked, but she'd deflected his attempts for them to get together. Part of the problem was she didn't know if she could be around him without blurting out the truth. Telling this man she was having his baby was something she wanted to do delicately. In the right way at the right time. And hopefully when she wasn't so scared of his reaction.

But in the meantime, avoiding him was just plain dumb.

That decided, she picked up the phone and called his office.

"Hi," she said, when the receptionist answered. "I'm Crissy Phillips, a friend of Josh's. Ah, Dr. Daniels. I wondered what his schedule looked like. If he was available for lunch."

"Oh, it's you!" the woman squealed. "I can't believe you're calling. We couldn't believe it when Dr. Josh told us he was dating. Finally. This is so exciting. You have to come by. I don't know if he'll have time for a long lunch, but he'll have a few minutes."

He talked about her? To his staff? She wasn't sure what to make of that, but decided it had to be a good thing. He wasn't exactly the kind of guy to share everything about his personal life. Which meant she was significant. At least that was going to be her interpretation of things.

"That sounds good," she said. "I'll come on over."

"I'm so glad. He really needs to see you. It's been a tough morning for him."

Which meant something had happened with one of his kids, she thought sadly.

"Thanks for telling me," she said. "Give me twenty minutes."

She parked across from the door to his offices and walked inside. The first thing she noticed was the bright colors of the walls. They were an ocean-blue—a fitting color considering the entire waiting-area walls were an underwater mural. There were fish and turtles and bits of seaweed. A diver lurked in a corner while four sharks played an intense game of volleyball by the window.

The overall effect was one of light and color. It was a cheerful, happy space, something his patients and their parents would appreciate.

The waiting room was empty. Crissy walked to the reception window where a young woman in a puppy-covered smock grinned at her.

"Ohmygod! You're Crissy, aren't you? I'm Natalie. I'm so excited to finally meet you."

Natalie turned and called out, "She's here, guys. Come meet her."

Three other woman clustered around the window. They introduced themselves so quickly, Crissy couldn't put names with faces.

"I go to your gym," one of them said. "The one across from the mall. I love it so much. No guys, which is the best. I work with a trainer and I've lost twenty pounds in just over two months. I'm trying to drag these slackers with me to one of the classes, but they're too lazy."

Natalie pulled a cookie out of her desk and waved it around. "Hey, I like my lifestyle just as it is. You're healthy enough for all of us."

"If you change your mind, we offer a free one-week membership," Crissy said. "You'd be welcome."

"Maybe." But Natalie looked doubtful. "Okay, we'll tell Dr. Josh you're here. It should just be a second."

Crissy took a seat, noting how a lot of the chairs were lower to the ground, probably so they would be more comfortable for the kids. There were plenty of toys lying around and a TV with a stack of DVDs next to it. She reached for a magazine and began flipping through it.

The front door opened and little girl walked in with her mother behind her. The child was maybe five or six and she wore a hat.

Natalie leaned out the reception window and grinned. "Why Heather Wilson, is that you? I swear you've grown an inch since you were last in here. Are you growing? Does your mother know about this?"

Heather giggled, then pulled off her hat. "Look!" she said proudly.

Short, blond curls covered her head. Natalie clapped her hands. "You have hair. Come see, everyone. Heather has hair!"

The office staff spilled into the waiting area and cooed over the little girl. While that was going on, the mother took a seat across from Crissy's.

"She's doing so well," the woman said with a relieved and happy smile.

"I can see that. She's beautiful."

The mother nodded. "We'd hoped, of course, for a miracle. But everyone told us it wasn't possible. That with her kind of cancer..." She swallowed. "I nearly lost hope. Then someone told us about Dr. Josh. He said there was a chance and he was right. The long nights in the hospital were a nightmare. But he was always there. It could be four in the morning and he'd just pop in to check on us. I've never known anyone like him."

She paused. "I guess I'm trying to tell you that if anyone can save your child, he can. Don't give up hope."

"Oh," Crissy said, not sure how to deal with the misunderstanding. "I'm, ah, not... I don't have a child here."

"She's his girlfriend," Natalie offered helpfully.

The mother laughed. "Really? That's great. He's been single far too long. We were all thinking he'd given up on love altogether. I'm glad he found someone."

Crissy smiled, even as she wondered if everyone on the planet had to know about her personal life.

"He's so caring and giving," the other woman continued. "Sometimes I think he's too good to be real."

Crissy knew for a fact that Josh was totally human. She'd seen him naked. But she understood the point being made. That he was one of the good guys.

A rush of longing filled her. Longing that they could work things out and that he could be the one. She cared about him more than she'd ever cared about another man. He was loving and compassionate, smart and funny. He could make her bones melt with just a smile. Wasn't that worth fighting for?

Little Heather came over and beamed. "I love Dr. Josh. He gives the bestest hugs. He always told me the truth. When it was gonna hurt, he didn't pretend it wasn't." She leaned forward. "I *hate* it when they tell me it's not gonna hurt and it does."

"I'm with you on that," Crissy told her.

Natalie leaned out of the reception window. "Okay, Crissy. You can come back now."

"Take your time," Heather's mother told her with a knowing smile. "We can wait."

Crissy had no idea what to say to that, so she just waved and followed Natalie to a large corner office. Here the colors were more subdued, but the space was still bright and open. Instead of the usual degrees hanging on the wall, there were posters of animals, including horses, penguins and a family of meerkats.

Seconds after she'd been ushered inside, the door opened again and Josh joined her.

"I'd heard you were in the building," he said as he crossed to her and took her hand in his.

"Just me and Elvis," she teased. "I was heading this way and I thought I'd stop by. How are you?"

As she asked the question, she stared into his eyes and saw the shadows there.

"Never mind," she told him. "I can see for myself that something bad happened."

"A patient," he said sadly. "He was barely two. That's wrong on so many levels. I never know what to say to the parents. How do you say you're sorry for that?"

"You did everything you could," she said, knowing it was true.

He squeezed her hand tighter. "I need to do more. I need to be able to save all of them and I don't know how. I have equipment so complicated it would take a year to teach you how to use it. I can study cells and make predictions. I have access to cutting-edge medicine. But it's all crap. In the end, I can't save them all."

Her heart ached for him. "No one expects you to."

"Matt's mother did. She sat in this office with hope in her eyes and asked for a miracle. I didn't have one for her. She's a single mother. *Was* a single mother. She was barely making it but she put all her hopes and dreams into that little boy. And last night those dreams ended."

Crissy's eyes filled with tears. "You're not superhuman. You're just a man."

"A useless one," he said, his voice thick with pain. "I was with them at the end. We both held him and then he was gone." He glanced at the wall. "He liked the meerkats best."

His pain filled the room and made it hard for her to breathe. How could he keep going through this time after time? How was there anything left? What price did he pay for caring so much? Did each child he lost take him back to Stacey's death? After being in so much darkness, could there be any light at all?

He released her hand and stepped back. "I know why you've been avoiding me," he said flatly.

She started to protest that she hadn't been, then decided to spare them both the lie.

"I'm too intense," he said. "The past five minutes would be a perfect illustration of that. I'm scaring you off and I don't blame you for wanting to run."

Did he really think that? Did he worry about losing her or did he want her gone?

"I don't have any plans to run," she said quietly. "Unless you want me to."

"What? No. Crissy, sometimes my job is the best one on the planet and sometimes it's the seventh level of hell. I can't disconnect from what I do. It makes me want to crawl inside myself and never care again. But I do care, about the kids, about you. I can't stop thinking about you and I've tried. You haunt me."

She liked the sound of that. It gave her hope.

She stood on her tiptoes and kissed him on the mouth. "I'm haunting you in a good way, right? Not a scary, icky zombie way."

He smiled. "No zombies, I promise."

Her chest tightened. She wasn't ready to tell him about the baby, but she didn't want to give up, either.

"I can handle what you do," she said.

"Are you sure?"

She nodded.

"I don't want to drag you down," he told her. "It's not a good place to be."

"Maybe you should spend less time there."

"That happens when I'm with you."

"Good. So I was thinking of getting some fabulous takeout tonight. Want to join me?"

He kissed her slowly, thoroughly, claiming her with a passion that took her breath away. He used his mouth and his tongue until she was ready to get naked right there in front of the meerkats.

"About seven?" he asked as he pulled back.

"What? Oh, tonight. Yeah. Seven works."

He grinned. "You're looking a little wild-eyed."

"That would be your fault."

He pulled up the front of his white coat, grabbed her hand, then pressed it to his groin. He was hard, which made her want to whimper.

"You have something to answer for, too."

"Then you'll have to punish me later," she whispered, teasingly.

"You can count on it."

Josh arrived at Crissy's house a few minutes early. The need to see her was strong. Being around her made his life better and right now he could use a little of that.

She opened the door before he could knock and waved him in.

"I got Chinese," she said by way of greeting. "A very

traditional, but well-loved form of takeout. I thought I should ease you in to some of the weird stuff I eat."

"Like?"

She grinned. "Oh, honey, you don't want to know."

"I'm tough."

"No guy is that tough."

They stood in the foyer. She motioned to the living room. "Do you remember my place or should I give you a tour?"

Now it was his turn to grin. "I remember everything about being here."

It had been the night of the party for Hope. When he'd followed Crissy home to see how she'd coped with meeting Brandon for the first time. He'd stopped by to offer comfort, but he'd ended up being the one transformed.

A black and white cat strolled past them. Crissy bent down and scooped him up.

"I don't believe you two met formally before," she said. "This is King Edward. He has a great sense of humor, which is unusual in a cat."

The cat was large and hairy, with big green eyes. Josh wasn't much of a cat person, but he reached out to pat the animal.

"Hey, Eddie," he said.

Both Crissy and the cat stiffened.

"He doesn't like to be called that," she whispered. "We use his full name at all times."

"Okay. King Edward it is."

Eddie sniffed his fingers, then raised his chin slightly as if saying he could be scratched now. Josh obliged him.

"He likes you," Crissy said as she put the cat down. "That's unusual."

"I'm a likable guy."

"I keep hearing that from other sources. Your staff was very exited to meet me."

He remembered their questions after Crissy had left and how they'd all adored her. "I don't get out much."

"Apparently. I thought they were going to offer me money to keep seeing you."

"Would you take it?"

"I'm thinking of expanding again soon, so probably. I'll need the cash for financing." She linked her arm with his. "Come on. I want to impress you with my ability to ladle food onto plates and heat it in the microwave. It's an art form not enough people appreciate."

He let her lead him into her kitchen, where she settled him on a bar stool by the island.

"I talked to Abbey this afternoon," she said as she pulled cartons of Chinese food out of the refrigerator. "Brandon is still doing well, so I guess I can let that worry go. We did talk about how I could maybe spend the day with him. Or at least an afternoon. By myself. Just the two of us." She bit her lower lip. "The thought terrifies me. What do you think? Can I do it? I mean I know I can, but would I get through two or three hours all right?"

"You'll be fine."

"I hope so."

She continued talking, but he wasn't listening. As he stared at her he realized he wasn't here for dinner, or even for sex, although he had big plans in that department. He was here because he needed her. Being around her made him feel alive. She was laughter and light and he was tired of living in the dark.

Chapter Ten

Crissy paced the width of Rachel's classroom as her friend stacked colored paper.

"It's three hours," Crissy said, trying to keep the panic out of her voice. Three hours? It was a lifetime!

"I thought we'd go to one of the multientertainment venues. It's not my thing, so I did some research. The one I like best has laser tag, video games, bumper cars, go-karts, miniature golf and boat bumpers." She paused and grimaced. "I really don't want to get on a tiny boat in an oversize pool, but if Brandon insists, I'll suck it up and do it. Anyway, when we're tired of all the activities, we can get a pizza. Afterward we can stop by some batting cages and get him ready for the season. Assuming he plays baseball. Do you think he does? Or is he more a soccer guy? I never played soccer. I don't know very much about it."

Rachel looked at her and laughed. "Is that all? What about a movie?"

Crissy hadn't thought of that. "Do you think there's time?"

"No, there isn't time for a movie, you nut. There isn't time for half of what you have planned. Come on. We're talking about three hours. That's nothing."

"So speaks the kindergarten teacher," Crissy mumbled. "You're good with kids."

"You've hung with Brandon before. You'll be fine."

"I haven't hung out with him at all. We've barely spoken. Plus now he knows I'm his birth mother. Before I was just some adult. The stakes are higher now. He's going to have expectations and I don't know what they are. What if I let him down? What if he hates me?"

"Why would he? You're great." She shook her head. "I'm talking to a wall. Do me a favor and collect all the crayons lying around, then sort them into the six containers on the side table. There should be about the same amount in each container."

"You're just giving me busywork to distract me."

"Maybe. You're making yourself crazy for nothing. Look, you pick him up and drive to the game place. There's fifteen minutes. The same taking him home. So that's a whole half hour gone. Eating is another twenty minutes. Make that thirty, if you're ordering a pizza. We're talking about filling two hours. You have more than enough planned."

Crissy knelt on the floor and began picking up

crayons. "What if he hates being with me? What if I'm boring or uncool?"

"You're a grown-up. You're uncool by definition."

She hated the sound of that. "But I want to be cool."

"Sorry. That's not how it works."

Damn. "What do we talk about? I don't know anything about him. Not really."

"So ask," Rachel said, obviously amused by the entire situation. "Have him tell you about school. What classes he likes and what he doesn't. Does he want to play sports in high school? Is he into cars? What does he want to study in college, that sort of thing. Argue about baseball teams or football. You're making this way too hard."

"You're being annoyingly rational."

"It's the friend's job."

Crissy scrambled under a small desk and grabbed three more crayons. "I guess it will be okay. I wonder how long he'll play each video game. If I knew that I could calculate how much time that would use up."

"Stop! Relax. Take a breath."

"I can't breathe. I can't think. I can only panic."

Later, as Crissy walked to her car. She tried to think positive thoughts, but it was impossible. There were so many ways for her to fail with Brandon. She needed a better plan.

Inspiration struck as she drove down the 15 freeway. She activated her hands free cell phone and made a call.

"Hello?"

The low, male voice made her smile. "Hi, Josh. What are you doing Saturday afternoon?"

"Not much. Aren't you seeing Brandon?"

"Uh-huh. We're off to one of those big arcade places. Laser tag, go-karts, video games and pizza. Sound like fun?"

"Are you asking for me or for him?"

"Both. I was thinking having you along would make things easier."

"You were, were you?"

"Uh-huh. I happen to know you find me unbelievably sexy. There would be a reward in it later. A really good one."

"That's tempting."

She heard the amusement in his voice. "Come on. It'll be fun."

"Okay. You win. What time?"

Crissy felt as if an entire butterfly marching band was practicing in her stomach. She wanted to blame the symptoms on something easy like morning sickness, but she'd yet to feel the slightest bit different on the pregnancy front. Instead she was forced to deal with the ugly truth—she was terrified.

Not scared, not nervous, but down-to-the-bone terrified that she would do something to make Brandon hate her. Or worse, think she was stupid.

She tried telling herself that everything would be fine. She and Brandon got along great. As long as they were having fun, he would be too busy to think she was stupid. If only she could believe herself.

While their time together was nothing more than an afternoon of hanging out together, to her it felt like so much more. She felt as if her entire relationship with her son was on the line. That was enough to make anyone feel a little queasy.

She pulled up in front of Abbey and Pete's house. Before she could get all the way up the walk to the small porch, the front door opened and Brandon stepped out.

He looked as nervous as she felt. As she moved closer, she saw a little excitement in his eyes, but a lot of uncertainty. At least they had that in common.

"Hey," she said. "Ready for a fun-packed afternoon?"

"Sure."

They stared at each other in a moment of awkwardness. She sensed some kind of physical greeting was called for. The last time she'd stepped into this house, she'd just been a friend of the family. Now she was his birth mother. That had to rate some kind of contact. But hugging felt like pushing things and ignoring the issue seemed cold. Not knowing what else to do, Crissy offered her hand.

Brandon's relief was instant. He took it and they shook. Weird, she thought, but a start.

The front door opened and Josh stepped out.

"Hi," she said as their eyes met.

"Hi, yourself."

She had no trouble imagining all sorts of fabulous physical greetings with this man. A lot of them involved being naked—perhaps not the best idea under the circumstances, but something she would want to explore later.

His smile told her he had the same sort of thing on his mind.

She loved this man, she thought in that instant. The feelings had been growing so slowly and she'd been distracted by Brandon, among other things, so she hadn't had a chance to notice. But she loved him. He was who she'd always been waiting for.

But what would happen when he found out about the baby? Would everything work out or was there a long, ugly road of pain ahead?

"Uncle Josh is coming with us," Brandon said. "That's okay, isn't it?"

"I think it's a great idea," she told him, refusing to think about what might happen. Instead she would focus on today and spending time with her son. "With three of us, we can be our own laser tag team."

His eyes widened. "We're gonna play laser tag?"

"You bet. I'm thinking that we're going to kick some serious butt. What do you think?"

Brandon grinned. "They're going down."

"Fantastic Fun" was a multiacre complex with every possible way to spend money on a kid. Crissy had gone online and purchased a day pass, allowing them access to all the activities—except video games. While she had ideas about what she wanted to do, she wanted to give Brandon the chance to make some choices, too.

"Cool car," Brandon said as Crissy locked the vehicle.

She smiled at her BMW 330i. "It was a gift from me to me. Sort of a self-congratulations for a job well done with my business."

"Sweet ride," he said, sounding closer to sixteen than twelve.

"Don't get your hopes up," Josh said, grabbing the boy around the neck and rubbing his knuckles across his head. "You're a long way from driving."

"But when I get there, maybe I can borrow her car."

"Or maybe not," Crissy said, wincing at the thought of a new driver taking the BMW out for a joyride. "We'll have to wait and see how things go."

"I'm very responsible," Brandon said with a grin. "Just ask my mom." His humor faded. "My, ah, other mom."

Great. They weren't even across the parking lot and already they were in awkward land.

Crissy put her hand on his arm. "Brandon, Abbey *is* your mom. She'll always be your mom. I'm Crissy. Unless you have another name you want to call me." She paused for effect. "One that I would have to approve."

That earned her a sweet smile. "Okay. Crissy's good. For now."

"If you call her Queen Crissy, you might have a better chance with the car," Josh offered.

Crissy eyed him. "You're supposed to be neutral, big guy. Like Switzerland."

"All right, Uncle Josh," Brandon said. "Great idea. Queen Crissy. I like it."

They were still laughing when they walked inside.

After an intense discussion about where to start their fun, they decided on laser tag. Vests, goggles and laser guns were provided, along with a map of the course.

The three of them huddled together to scope out the competition.

"Them," Brandon said, pointing to a group of giggling teenage girls. "They aren't going to be into the game. They'll be slow and shoot bad. We can totally annihilate them."

"So speaks the compassionate member of our team," Crissy murmured, wanting to defend her gender, but knowing Brandon was right.

"We're here to win," he told her. "That family should be next." He pointed to a father, mother and two little boys about five and six. "They're too young to be good."

"Culling the weakest members of the herd," Josh whispered into her ear. "Your gene pool at work."

She grinned. "If we were still hunting the woolly mammoth, I'd want Brandon on my team."

"So would I."

They fleshed out the rest of their strategy, which included staying together to protect each other's backs, along with scouting expeditions to scope out any ringers in hiding.

Once inside the dusky corridors of the laser tag course, Crissy found herself getting seriously into the game. She no longer cared about defending her gender or giving the teenage girls a break. Instead she wanted the highest possible score.

They moved purposefully, staying together. The corridor opened into three possible routes.

"On your right," Crissy yelled, seeing movement in that direction.

Both Josh and Brandon turned and fired. Crissy instinctively turned the other way in time to fire on the father of the family.

Twenty minutes later they pored over their score sheet. Their total hits as a team was more than double anyone else's in the maze with them.

"Not that we had a lot of competition," Crissy said. "Brandon, you did great. Look at your number of shots and your number of hits. Your accuracy is just over eighty percent. Josh, you're barely at sixty percent. You're going to have to be on probation."

"I have other skills," he muttered, then took the sheet from her. "What about you, missy? You think you're so hot and… Oh."

Brandon grinned. "Look, Uncle Josh. She kicked our butt. Jeez, Crissy, your accuracy is higher than mine and you got off more shots."

"I'm competitive," she said primly. "Don't mess with me during a game."

"I guess not," Josh said. "I think it's time to even things up. Now we're going to play a game that I can win at, what with being a doctor and all."

Crissy groaned. "No way. It's boring."

"It's a game of skill and patience. I have both."

"What's he talking about?" Brandon asked.

"Golf," she said with a sigh. "Or in this case, miniature golf."

Twenty minutes later, Josh was kicking both their butts.

"It's all his putting practice," Crissy told Brandon. "We can't compete against that. Those doctors and their golf games."

Although in Josh's case, his victory had to be about something other than his skill at golf. She happened to know that he rarely took time off and that he didn't play much golf. His patients got nearly all his attention.

They stood on the fifth hole and faced the slow moving windmill.

"The trick with this one is timing," Josh said confidently. "Watch how the blades move. You'll need to shoot between them."

"Are they really called blades?" Crissy asked. "Aren't they something else?"

"I have no idea."

"We could go back to my place and look it up on the computer."

Josh patted her shoulder. "Sorry, no. We're staying through the whole game. A game, I would like to point out, you're losing."

"I hate this game. It's stupid."

Brandon grinned at her. "Come on, Crissy. You have to learn how to lose gracefully."

"Never. I pout when I lose."

They made it through the turning blades and down onto the second level of the hole. Crissy had been nervous about spending time with Brandon, but everything was going smoothly. He was easy to be with, she thought. A fun, funny, smart kid. Her kid.

She felt a tightness inside. A longing and a powerful sense of regret. If only...

She shook her head. If only what? If only she'd kept Brandon? If she had, he wouldn't be this charming boy. He would be someone else. Who he was now was a result of Pete and Abbey's influence. They had done so much for him. She would always be grateful. Yes, she had regrets, but they were selfishly about her. Knowing all she knew now, she wouldn't wish for anything better for her son.

He caught her looking at him and smiled. She smiled back.

"I talked to Mom about what you said," he told her. "About giving me up for adoption. I know you were trying to tell me that it wasn't about me."

Her good mood evaporated. Oh God. Was he emotionally scarred? Angry? Depressed?

"It wasn't," she said. "Do you understand that?"

"Yeah. She explained it real well. She said it was like the difference between me, Emma and Hope. They're a lot younger than me and can't do stuff I can do. When they get older, they'll be better at it, you know. You were young when you got pregnant. You didn't know how to be a mom or raise a kid. It would have been hard for you and not very good for me. So you found someone who was ready to have a baby."

He shrugged. "It worked out for the best. I love my mom and dad. Now that you're older, you can cope with me and we can be friends."

He sounded so rational and together, she thought, amazed and more grateful to Abbey than she could say.

"So we're okay?" she asked.

He grinned. "Uh-huh. But Uncle Josh is going to brag about beating us for the rest of the day."

"We can't let that happen. We'll try harder."

"There's no point," Josh said smugly. "I'm in my element."

The rest of the time flew by. Crissy couldn't believe

it when she glanced at her watch and saw they were already ten minutes late returning Brandon. She called Abbey who was delighted the outing had gone so well, then herded both guys to her car and drove back.

When they reached the house, Brandon jumped out. "That was fun," he said. "Can we do it again?"

"Absolutely. I was thinking one weekend we could go to an Angels game."

His eyes lit up. "That would be great. I love baseball."

"Me, too."

He ran around the car and threw his arms around her. Slowly, carefully, she hugged him back.

He was tall and skinny, all bones and muscle. Not a little boy anymore but still her child. Emotions flooded her—mostly good ones, with a hint of sadness for what could never be recovered, even if she didn't want it to be. Then he was running up to the house and going inside.

"You okay?" Josh asked.

Crissy nodded as she blinked. "I'm not going to cry. I'm not sad at all. I'm happy. It was just a lot to take in."

"He likes you."

"I like him."

"You're going to be good for him. You'll be someone he can go to for advice. When he grows up, he'll talk about you to his kids and they'll hear the love in his voice when he does."

She swallowed. "Trying not to cry here. You could help by not saying stuff like that."

"Sorry."

But he didn't sound sorry. He sounded pleased.

"Thanks for coming along," she told him. "I was so scared."

"I know, but it worked out."

"Because you were there. It would have been awkward otherwise."

He moved close and kissed her on the forehead. "You're doing great. Trust your instincts."

"I will."

He glanced at his watch. "I need to swing by the hospital. I want to check on a couple of kids. What are you going to do?"

"Go thank Abbey for everything, then head home."

"I'll call you later."

"I'd like that."

When he'd driven off, Crissy walked up to the house and knocked on the front door. Abbey let her in.

"Brandon can't stop talking about what a great time he had with you. You've made a fan."

Crissy impulsively hugged her. "Because of you, Abbey. I can't thank you enough. You've been great."

Abbey hugged her back, then waved her toward the kitchen. "I'll take the praise because I like it, but you're making too big a deal out of this. I just did what anyone else would do."

"I don't think so. You've been amazingly generous. Brandon told me what you said to him, about why I gave him up for adoption. He understood perfectly. You always know exactly what to say."

"I wish." She walked over to the sink and washed her

hands, then dried them, rubbed them with flour and began kneading dough.

Crissy had heard about the process of baking bread, but she'd never seen it before. "You do that a lot, don't you?"

"A couple of times a week. It's how I relax."

"I go for a jog or eat ice cream."

"I can get behind the ice cream suggestion. As for the whole jogging thing…" Abbey paused, frowned, then shook her head. "Nope. Never jogged in my life. I have no real plans to change that, either."

"You have other qualities." Crissy sat on the stool by the island. "You didn't have to be so nice."

"Neither did you. We're all delighted this is working out. Brandon needs you and I think you need him."

Crissy could agree with the latter, even as she questioned the former. But she liked the sound of being needed by her son, so she would go with it.

"I have a question," she said, wondering if she was about to be incredibly personal and/or rude. "But if you don't want to answer it, you don't have to."

"That sounds intriguing," Abbey teased. "Unfortunately my life isn't that interesting, so I'm going to guess your question isn't about me."

"It's about Josh."

"And?"

Crissy looked at her. "He's wonderful with his patients. I've seen him interact with them. He's great with your kids. But when he and I were talking, he said he didn't want children of his own. What do you know about that?"

Abbey sighed. "He said that?"

Crissy nodded.

"I was hoping it was just a phase he would get over, but apparently not."

"A phase?"

"I'm being a horrible person," Abbey said. "I know that, so just go with it. The no-children thing is because of Stacey. She couldn't have children. Something I can relate to. When Josh told me, I thought it might be something we could bond over. You know, a shared experience to bring us closer."

"You weren't close?"

Abbey hesitated. "Not really. I didn't… Let's just say Stacey wasn't my favorite person."

"You're kidding. I thought she was a saint or something. Josh met her while she was visiting sick kids in the hospital."

"Drama queen is more like it," Abbey muttered. "Okay, forget I said that. Stacey had to deal with a lot of tragedy in her life. She was sick and knew that when the cancer came back it would kill her. That's enough to make anyone wonky. But she carried it to the extreme. I had problems when I was younger, but you don't hear me talking about them. I'm healthy and I want to live my life. But not her. Talking to Stacey was like living in a gothic novel. Everything was doom and gloom. When I mentioned adoption, she refused to discuss it. It was too wrong for her to take in a child when she could be dead by morning on any given day."

Abbey dropped her chin to her chest. "I sound awful. I know I do. Stacey went through so much more than anyone should. She suffered greatly and in the end, the cancer came back and killed her. It's just…it's almost as if…" She looked at Crissy. "I swear I'm going to hell, but it's almost as if she was happy when it did. Like it proved everything she'd said."

Crissy didn't know what to think. This picture of Stacey wasn't at all like the saint she'd thought Josh had married. And speaking of Josh…

"What did he have to say about Stacey's behavior?"

"He's a guy." Abbey rolled her eyes. "He was crazy in love with her sweet spirit and frailness. He got to take care of her, which he seemed to like. Every moment was precious, because it might be their last. Honestly? It made me mad. Before Stacey, Josh never said he didn't want kids. It had never come up in conversation, but I figured he was like Pete—ready for a big family. But once Stacey was in his life, he claimed he never wanted children. It was all about her."

Crissy was still taking it all in. "I don't know what to think. I'd wondered if his attitude might be about Stacey, but does that make it better or worse? Is admitting he wants children now a betrayal of Stacey and if it is, will he let himself?"

"I don't know," Abbey admitted. "But if you're asking the question, I'm assuming things are getting serious."

"A little. Maybe. I like him. He's a great guy. I want to believe we have a future."

Abbey laughed. "If I didn't have dough hands, I'd hug you right now. This is great. I was hoping the two of you would get together more permanently. You're exactly the kind of woman Josh should be with. And he's a great guy. Next to Pete, he's about as good as they come."

"Next to Pete?"

"I can't help that I married the best."

Crissy smiled, then let the smile fade. "There are so many complications. His work, his past, the kids thing. I want a family."

"I really think he does, too," Abbey said. "The big question is will he let himself admit that? I don't have an answer. The good news is you have time on your side."

Less than she thought. Crissy was going to tell Josh in the next week or so. Which meant he would have to get over his past really fast or they would be dealing with it.

"What?" Abbey asked. "You're thinking something."

"It's not important."

"It looked important. Am I prying?"

"No, I just don't want to put you in the middle."

"Of… Oh. You and Josh. But how could I?" Her mouth dropped opened. "Oh! You're…are you pregnant?"

Crissy wasn't sure if she was happy or sorry Abbey knew. "You're going to have to keep it quiet for a few days. Until I tell him."

Abbey beamed. "But you are. Pregnant! That's wonderful."

"I'm not so sure," Crissy admitted. "I mean I'm thrilled about the baby. I want to start a family. But now? Like this? I don't know what Josh is going to think. He might be furious or feel I trapped him or something."

"Did you?"

"Of course not."

"Then don't worry about it. He'll understand."

Crissy wasn't so sure.

"There's also the complication of Brandon. What is he going to think when he finds out I'm pregnant again but this time I'm keeping the baby? Won't he feel rejected all over again?"

Abbey sighed. "I hadn't thought about that. We'll talk about it and he'll understand. It may take a bit, but he'll get it. He really cares about you."

For how long? "I didn't mean to make this much trouble for everyone."

"A baby is never trouble," Abbey said. "It's a miracle. It's time you found that out for yourself. As for Josh, I know it's scary to think how he might react. But give him a chance. Maybe he'll surprise you in a good way."

"I hope so."

They talked for a few more minutes, then Crissy left. She'd barely turned the corner when her cell phone rang. She pushed the voice activation button on her steering wheel.

"Hello?"

"Crissy? It's Dev. We're at the hospital. Noelle's having the baby."

Rachel and Carter were already in the waiting room when Crissy arrived. Rachel raced over. "She's close. Really close. They've taken her into delivery. She looked good and she says it's not so bad." Rachel's fingers dug into her arm. "Tell me it's not so bad."

"You'll be fine. They have drugs if the pain gets bad."

"Right. Drugs."

Carter took her free hand in his. "Come on. Relax. You're a long way from giving birth. It will be fine."

"You don't actually know that. It's easy to be all calming and superior when you're not planning on passing a bowling ball through a pinhead in a few months."

"Point taken."

Crissy laughed. Being around Carter and Rachel was always a fun time. They, like Noelle and Dev, were a perfect couple. Watching them together made the world seem like a better place.

Rachel looked at her. "Do you remember anything from when you had Brandon?"

"Not really. It was fairly quick. I was scared and I just wanted it over."

She'd been so young, she thought sadly. Even though her mother had been with her, along with Abbey, she'd felt alone. Probably the guilt talking. Now, looking back on that teenager, she could be more compassionate.

"She'll be fine," Rachel said, almost chanting. "I'll be fine, you'll be fine. So much fineness. Fine. Fine. Fine."

Carter looked at Crissy and mouthed "Help!"

Crissy nodded and took Rachel's arm. "Come on, you. Let's take a walk. Remember how you mocked me about my terror at spending three hours with Brandon? I'm going to return the favor. You'll love it."

Rachel groaned. "I didn't even ask. How was it? Did everything go okay?"

"It was great." Crissy led her into the corridor. "We talked, we bonded. I'm really happy. I think he and I are going to have a great relationship."

"So that's good, right?"

"Uh-huh."

Crissy distracted her with idle talk until they reached the nursery. Rachel touched the glass separating her from the newborns and sighed.

"Look at them. They're so beautiful. Those tiny little faces. They're all wrapped up. I read about that. It's to make them feel safe, like they were in the womb. Oh, I want a baby."

Me, too, Crissy thought. "You're having one. In just a few months."

Rachel touched her stomach and smiled. "Hurry up, little one. We want to see you."

"Better?" Crissy asked.

"Much. The panic has totally faded."

Carter rounded the corner and hurried toward them. "She had the baby. A girl. Everything is good. Dev looks pale but proud. Noelle says as soon as she gets to her room you're to come right in and you can hold little Mindy yourselves."

It was early evening by the time Crissy pulled up in front of Josh's town house. They'd spoken on the phone earlier and she'd told him about the baby. He'd invited her over for dinner…and breakfast. An invitation she couldn't refuse.

As she walked up to the front door, she found she couldn't stop smiling. Holding Noelle's newborn had been an incredible experience.

"You look happy," Josh said as he opened the door. "Everything okay with the new family?"

"It's perfect." She stepped inside and kissed him. "Noelle sailed through delivery with no problems. Mindy is beautiful and perfect. I had no idea babies smelled so good. They let me hold her and I never wanted to give her back."

Josh's expression didn't change, which made her wonder what he was thinking. This seemed like a good a time as any to find out...and to tell the truth.

"I'm just about to start dinner," he said. "I didn't know when you'd be coming by."

"Before you do, I need to tell you something."

His gaze never left hers. "A good something or a bad something?"

"I think it's the best. I hope you will, too." Now that she'd picked the moment, she didn't know what to say.

"Crissy?"

"Right. I should talk. The thing is neither of us is to blame. We were caught off guard by the moment. It happened. We should have planned better, but we didn't. Oh, damn. I'm not saying this right. I guess the biggest point is that I'm happy. So happy. Delighted, bordering on giddy."

She took both his hands in hers. "I'm pregnant, Josh. From that first night we were together. We're having a baby."

Chapter Eleven

Josh stared at Crissy. He felt as if he were underwater. He couldn't seem to move and nothing looked right.

Then it hit him—a crushing weight of guilt. It slammed into him, knocking the breath out of him. He couldn't have a child with Crissy. It was wrong on more levels than he could count.

Without having to close his eyes, he saw Stacey in the room. The hurt in her eyes, the sadness in her expression. A child with someone else? What right did he have to experience that when she'd never been able to?

Time bent and it was years before he'd married her. Back when he'd proposed three times and been turned down each time.

Finally he'd cornered her, emotionally and physically. "What the hell is your problem?" he'd asked, angry by her constant refusal, the anger hiding his pain at being rejected by the only woman he'd ever loved.

She'd faced him, her violet eyes dark with tears, her mouth quivering. "I can't give you a child," she whispered, her voice so quiet, he'd had to strain to hear her. "I'm not physically capable of carrying a child to term. I don't think it's right to adopt when the cancer could return at any time. You want to have a real family and I can't give you that. Go be with someone who can."

At that moment he'd known her greatest fear was being rejected for her physical imperfections. On the outside, she was as beautiful as an angel, but on the inside, she had been twisted by a disease that couldn't be controlled.

"I don't want children."

He'd said the words without thinking, yet as soon as he spoke them, he knew them to be true. They felt right.

"I don't want children," he repeated with conviction. "I want you."

It had taken him nearly two months to convince her he meant what he said. Only then, when she was sure she wasn't taking anything from him, had she said yes.

The past bent, then snapped. He was left staring at Crissy, at her expression of happiness and delight. Emotions he could never share on this topic.

"No," he said firmly, knowing he couldn't will the child away. "I don't want a child with you."

She gasped and took a step back.

"What the hell were you thinking?" he demanded. "How could you do this? Did you plan it? Are you trying to trap me?"

"What?"

The entire situation was wrong. He got that now. He should never have gone out with her, cared about her. He didn't have the right.

"Are you crazy?" She glared at him. "Why would I want to trap you? I don't need a man in my life. This just happened. Don't you remember that first night we were together? *You* came to me. *You* walked into my house to find out if I was all right. So what exactly would my plan have been? After twelve years I realized that the son I'd given up for adoption had an uncle who didn't want children. Perfect, I thought. Now I'll get involved with the family, act all broken so he'll come over, seduce me and then I can have his baby?"

He knew she was telling the truth—that his charge was ridiculous. So why did he feel so compelled to make it? Why did he want to lash out at her?

"If anyone was doing the using around here, it was you," she told him, putting her hands on her hips and glaring. "You'd been doing without for a long, long time. You got an itch and decided to use me to scratch it. Don't come crying to me because you forgot to use protection and you got caught."

More guilt filled him, but this time it had nothing to do with Stacey. Crissy was right about the itch. He'd never meant to use her but a case could be made that he had.

"Crissy," he began.

She cut him off. "No, Josh. You don't get to say all those things to me and then expect everything to be fine. We're having a baby. Doesn't that mean anything to you?"

"It means you finally get what you want. You regretted giving up Brandon and now you have someone to take his place."

"What?"

"It's true. I'll agree that I have to take responsibility for the pregnancy. My excuse is I haven't had to deal with birth control in nearly ten years. Stacey couldn't have children. It wasn't an issue. As I haven't been with anyone else since she died, I don't think about keeping condoms around. What's your excuse? You date. Why weren't you prepared?"

She pressed her lips together. "I just wasn't."

"Great reason. You might want to think of a better one. Maybe you did see this as an opportunity to have the child you now want. Who cares if I didn't want to take that on? This is all a game to you and I'm not playing."

"A game? It's never been that. I can't believe you're accusing me of having an ulterior motive. As far as I'm concerned, we're equally responsible. You don't want kids. Fine. You don't have to have them. Here's a newsflash. I don't need you to have this baby. I'm more than willing to sign anything you want saying you give up your rights and I give up the right to child support. Does that make it better?"

"It's not that simple." Even though he wanted it to be.

"Sure it is. I'm more than prepared to be a single mother."

"For how long? You've made a career out of running from your emotional responsibilities."

She flinched as if he'd hit her and he knew then he'd crossed the line. That he'd damaged whatever had existed between them.

"I don't get it," she said slowly. "I thought you were the best kind of man. I thought you were amazing and kind and loving. I knew you still loved Stacey, but I thought that was about having a heart that didn't let go. I see now you were just masquerading as someone I thought I could love. In reality you're nothing more than a cruel, selfish bastard. I don't regret being pregnant. I want this baby. I just wish you weren't the father."

She picked up her purse and walked out the door. When it slammed shut behind her, he was left alone.

By Saturday morning Crissy knew she had to snap out of her mood funk, for the health of the baby if nothing else. She felt lost and unfocused, and there was an ache inside that refused to go away.

She hated that she kept waiting for Josh to call and say it had been a horrible mistake. That he'd momentarily been possessed by aliens and in truth he was delighted about the baby and longed to be with both their child and her. That he loved her with a fierceness that defied description. Barring that, she would accept a decent apology.

Neither was forthcoming.

She tried to focus on her work, because at least that was a distraction, but she couldn't find her usual joy in her business.

"Things will get better," she told herself. They had to, right?

Finally, unable to stand just sitting around and moping, she went into the small bathroom attached to her office and changed into the workout clothes she kept on site. She was nearly out the door when the phone rang. It was her private line.

She hated the sudden burst of hope in her chest and how much she longed to hear Josh's voice. Where was her pride and sense of self-preservation? Was she one of those stupid women who let herself be emotionally beat up by the same guy over and over again?

Apparently, she thought grimly as she hurried back to her desk and grabbed the phone.

"Hello?"

"It's Abbey. I hope I'm not disturbing you, but I have a handsome guy standing here who wants to ask you something."

"Mo-om!"

The disgusted tone was audible and made her smile. Okay, so it wasn't Josh, but it was still a call she wanted to take.

"Am I embarrassing you?" Abbey asked cheerfully.

"You know you are. You like embarrassing me."

"I kind of do. Here you go."

"Hey, Crissy."

"Good morning," she said, happy to hear her son's voice. "What's up in your world?"

"Not much. Look, Emma is at her girlfriend's house and Dad's taking Hope to some stupid petting zoo. They asked me to go with them." He sounded outraged. "To a petting zoo. I'm practically a teenager."

"Horrifying."

"Yeah. Anyway, do you want to come over for lunch? We have leftover Chinese from last night and it's really good. I thought we could hang out for a while."

Some of her pain eased. "I'd like that a lot."

They settled on a time. Five minutes later Crissy cranked up the incline on a treadmill and set the speed to six miles an hour. Between now and her lunch date, she was going to run away from her problems.

"Dad thinks I should be a doctor, like Uncle Josh," Brandon said between bites of Kung Pao Chicken. "I don't know. I want to play baseball. I guess you can't play forever. Guys get old and stuff. I could always be a doctor then."

"The medical profession will love knowing it's your fallback position," Crissy teased. "Depending on how long you play baseball, you could be really old when you go to medical school. Like maybe thirty."

Brandon shrank back in his chair. "Thirty? Can you still learn stuff then?"

"Those of us in our thirties muddle through," Abbey said. "There are people in college in their seventies."

He rolled his eyes. "Why? They're not going to get a job or anything."

"Some people like to learn things because learning is fun and interesting," Abbey said. "Some people like school."

Brandon looked as confused as if she'd just spoken Mandarin.

"Don't you like school?" Crissy asked.

He shrugged. "Most of the time. I like math and science. I like to read, but not as much as Emma. If she could be a book, she'd be really happy. History is dumb and I hate writing papers."

"Typical jock," Abbey murmured, then looked at Crissy. "I totally blame you for that. You're so athletic. And his birth father was a jock. Couldn't you have fallen for someone intellectual?"

Crissy laughed. "Sorry. Next time I'm in high school and getting in trouble, I'll choose someone different."

"It can't be helped now," Abbey said, looking at her son.

Brandon laughed. "Come on, Mom. You love me just the way I am. You don't want me to be different."

"Oh, I don't know. A son who cleans his room could be exciting. At least it would be a change."

He sighed heavily. "I'll clean my room. I promise."

"The deadline is Sunday by one. And yes, we're going to church, so don't think you can use that time to do it."

He picked up his plate and carried it to the counter. "I guess I should go do it now, huh?"

Abbey shrugged. "It's your call. Your room—your responsibility."

He turned to Crissy. "See what she's like?"

"You're pretty lucky and you know it."

He grinned. "I'm not saying that." Then he ran out of the room.

Crissy watched him go. "You're amazing with him."

"He makes it easy. Which is also your responsibility."

"I guess I don't mind taking the credit, even though I don't deserve it."

Abbey passed over the container of pot stickers. "How are you doing? You seem…I don't know. Tired maybe."

"I have a lot on my mind. Before I forget, I wanted to ask your opinion about Brandon and the baby." Crissy glanced toward the doorway to make sure they were still alone. "Telling him. I was thinking of waiting until I'm showing a little. Eight months before the actual birth seems excessive. What do you think?"

"I agree. Waiting isn't a problem. He'll still have plenty of time to deal with the situation."

"Do you think it's going to be hard for him?" Crissy asked. "I worry about that. About him thinking I didn't care about him, but I care about this child."

"I don't know how he'll handle it," Abbey told her. "But I do know we'll tell him together, in a supportive environment and that we'll get through whatever his reaction is. We're his family and he knows that. I have a feeling everything is going to be fine."

Crissy hoped she was right. "Have you talked to Josh?"

"Not in a few days. He hasn't been around. What—" Abbey grimaced. "You told him, didn't you? From the look on your face, I'm going to guess it didn't go well."

"It was a disaster." Crissy set down her fork. "I don't get it. I thought I knew him. I thought we had a connection that mattered to him. He totally freaked. He accused me of tricking him so that I could get pregnant. Worse, he flat out said he didn't want a child with me."

She did her best to stay strong as she spoke the words, but it was hard. Emotions welled up inside of her, making her hurt again.

"He didn't mean that," Abbey said.

"He sounded fairly sure."

"He thinks he means it, which isn't the same thing. You have to know he's reacting to his past rather than to you, right?"

"Even if that's true, does it matter? If he can't let go of the past, then we don't have a chance. I really thought he was the one."

Tears filled her eyes. She did her best to blink them away.

"I thought he was great," Crissy went on. "The guy you wait your whole life to meet. Now I'm not so sure. Did I make him what I wanted him to be? Did I create the perfect man out of a normal guy with a few problems. Everyone has problems—I'm good with that. But I'm not sure I can handle Josh's. I'll never be Stacey. And until he's willing to let her go, he can't be someone I can love and he won't be a father to our child."

Abbey bit her lower lip. "I'm so sorry. I hate that this is happening. I know in my heart that Josh has to be excited about the baby."

"If he is, he's doing a heck of a job convincing me otherwise."

"Don't be mad at him," Abbey said. "This is all my fault."

"I can't wait to hear how."

"That first night you were here, I could see he was attracted to you. He hadn't dated since Stacey's death and I was getting on him about going out more. I told him to find someone and have sex before he forgot how. I just didn't think he would do it that night."

Crissy smiled. "I hate to burst your bubble of self-importance, but you have nothing to do with what happened. As much as Josh adores you, he wouldn't go out and have sex just because you told him to."

"I want to believe that," Abbey said, looking miserable.

"Does he ever do what you say?"

"Oh." Her expression cleared. "Not really."

"Why would he this time?"

"I like your logic," Abbey told her. "But that doesn't solve the problem. Give him time. I think he'll come around."

"I hope so," Crissy murmured, knowing she would love for Josh to be a part of the baby's life, not to mention her own. But only if he did so with an open heart.

"Are you nervous about the baby?" Abbey asked.

"A little. So far I'm not thinking much about being pregnant. It's so new that I—"

She stopped talking when Abbey held up her hand. The other woman put her fingers to her lips and quietly rose. She moved to the doorway and looked down the hall, then returned to the table.

"Sorry," she said. "I thought I heard a noise. Brandon found out you were his birth mother by listening in on a conversation between Pete and me. It's kind of a thing with him, and we're doing our best to break him of the habit."

"I'm glad you checked," Crissy said. "This isn't how I want him to find out he's going to have a half brother or sister."

"Agreed. Anyway, you were saying you were in denial about the baby."

"Not denial exactly, but I'm not thinking about it every minute. I'm okay with being a single mother, at least intellectually. I'm financially secure, I have a support group, I run my own company, so my hours can be as flexible as I want them to be."

"You have me," Abbey said. "I want to be considered part of your support group. I've raised three babies, so I'm experienced with the whole newborn thing."

"I'm happy to hear that. You're my total mother role model."

Abbey smiled. "You're sweet to say so, but I've made mistakes. Pete helps a lot, too. He's great with the kids."

"I want Josh to be like that," Crissy admitted. "I want him to be excited and involved. I can't believe he would walk away from his own child."

"He won't," Abbey told her. "Like I said—give him time."

But would time be enough? "It won't work if he's not willing to move on," she said slowly. "Which can be harder than it should be. I felt so guilty about giving up Brandon, I didn't let myself move on for years. What if Josh is the same way? If he takes too long, he'll lose so much with the baby."

"Are you willing to give him a chance?" Abbey asked.

"Of course. I love him. But he has to be willing to take a chance, too."

Tommy was seven and totally into airplanes. He wanted to be a commercial pilot when he grew up, but that was only after flying fighter jets for the air force. He already knew more about planes than Josh did and he wanted to go to an air show for his eighth birthday.

Josh's job was to make sure he lived until that birthday.

He checked Tommy's chart, then walked into his room. There were posters of airplanes on the wall and several stuffed animals piled on the bed. Tommy's mother slept in the bed next to her son's and even in sleep, she looked exhausted.

Josh moved quietly, not wanting to bother either of them. As he reached out to lightly touch Tommy's face, he braced for the heat of a fever brought on by the aggressive chemo he had prescribed.

It was a classic choice of two evils. If Tommy didn't have the chemo, his cancer would kill him. But the chemo was almost a death sentence itself. Symptoms varied, but in this child it had produced raging fevers that kept spiking at terrifying temperatures.

There was an ice bath kept at the ready and in the past thirty-six hours, the nurses had used it twice.

His fingers brushed against cool, damp skin. Josh frowned. Damp? Why would—

Not daring to hope, he gently pulled back the covers and saw Tommy's pajamas plastered to his body. They were soaked, as was the bedding.

"Hot damn!" he said, louder than he meant to. Tommy's mother opened her eyes and sat up.

"What happened?" she asked, already on her feet and moving to her son. "Is it his fever? Should I call the nurse?"

He grabbed her hand and put it on Tommy's thin chest. In the light spilling in from the corridor, he saw her face transform from terror to wonder.

"The fever's broken," she whispered. "It's broken. That's good, right?"

"It's better than good. It means he beat the chemo and he'll be all right. I'll have the nurse come in to change his bed and check his temperature, but it's way down."

"Thank you," she said, then put her hand over her mouth as tears trickled down her cheeks. "Thank you. No one else would take a chance on him. You've saved him."

"Not yet," he told her. "But we're in a much better place than we were."

He started to leave. She grabbed his coat sleeve and held him in place.

"You always do this," she said. "Come here in the middle of the night. I want you to know how much that means to us. I'm sure it makes your wife crazy, so would you please tell her thank you from my husband and me? Remind her what a great guy she married. While you're at it, tell your kids they're lucky to have you for their dad."

He nodded because there was no point in telling her he wasn't married and didn't have any children. Instead he went to the nursing station to request they change Tommy's bed, then he wrote the results of his visit in the boy's chart.

It was late and the hospital was about as quiet as it ever got. He was exhausted. At home he could go to bed, even if he couldn't sleep. He hadn't been sleeping much since Crissy had told him about the baby. But trying to rest made sense. Still, instead of heading for the parking garage, he took the elevator down two floors and walked toward the newborn nursery.

There were seven infants sleeping in their bassinets. Just beyond the glass wall, he saw a nurse rocking a fussy baby. She moved with an age-old rhythm that was as instinctive as breathing.

He had loved his wife with a passion he'd thought would live forever. Her passing had nearly destroyed him. So now, four years later, did he have the right to start over?

He hated that he even had to ask the question, but he couldn't help himself. In the darkness, when he was alone and there was no one around, he could admit that yes, a part of him did want a child. His child. Crissy's child.

If he were to pick any woman in the world to be his baby's mother, she would be the one. He admired so many things about her and he knew she would be fiercely loving and nurturing.

She was also an innocent party in all this and he owed her an apology. He'd been wrong in his accusations, lashing out because he'd been stunned by her announcement.

How was he supposed to reconcile what had happened with Crissy with his relationship with Stacey? He'd told Stacey he didn't want children and he'd meant it. But if he admitted he wanted this child with Crissy, didn't that make everything about his marriage a lie? Didn't that make him a bastard?

How could he deal with the guilt and find peace? How could he be the man Crissy and his baby deserved?

There were no answers in the night. Just the sleeping newborns and the ache in his chest that told him he very much wanted to be a father and damn the consequences.

Chapter Twelve

Josh waited until the next morning before going to Crissy's house. He thought about calling first, but had the feeling she might refuse to see him. After what he'd said before, he'd earned her anger.

So he showed up at seven-thirty with Starbucks coffee and a bag of scones. She answered after the first ring.

She was in the perfect state of almost-ready when women are most beautiful. Her makeup was on, but she wore a robe instead of a suit. Hot rollers covered her head and she had a brush in her hand.

He'd been in pain since she told him about the baby, but this time, when he looked at her and felt the ache, it had a very different cause. He ached because he wanted her. Not just in his bed, but in his life. He wanted to talk to her and share dreams with her. He wasn't prepared to say he loved her, but with time, that could come, too.

"I have a meeting this morning," she said by way of greeting. "I don't have a lot of time."

"Then I'll talk fast. Can I come in?"

She eyed the coffee. "I'm supposed to stay away from caffeine."

"I brought you decaf."

"In theory a good thing," she muttered, taking it from him and stepping aside so he could enter her house.

He followed her into the kitchen and set down the scones. She shoved her brush into her robe pocket and turned to face him.

"What do you want?"

Not exactly the response he'd hoped for but he knew he was going to have to earn his way back to her good side.

"I want to apologize," he said, trying to put as much conviction in his voice as possible. "My reaction to your announcement was wrong in more ways than I can count. I know you didn't set me up. It was ridiculous for me to go there. I was wrong to accuse you of running away from responsibilities. I'm sure there are other things I said that I shouldn't have and I apologize for them as well. I'm sorry, Crissy. I mean it."

She stared at him for a long time, then looked down at her coffee. "It's not that simple, Josh. I know I'm supposed to accept your apology so that everything could be fine between us, but that would be a lie. I hate what you said and even more, I hate that you thought it in the first place. I'm not the kind of woman who tricks men. Why don't you know that?"

"I do. I reacted out of a lot of stuff that has nothing to do with you. My past. Issues with Stacey. That all crashed in on me."

She raised her head and stared at him. "You're wrong. All that stuff *does* have something to do with me. Your past makes you who you are. It will always affect me."

She was right. She was the kind of woman who would always be right. It could make a guy crazy, if he let it. Josh planned on enjoying the ride.

"I can't change my past, but I can learn to manage it better," he said. "As to the pregnancy, I know we're equally responsible. Neither of us was thinking that night. Now there are consequences and I want you to know I'm prepared to be a part of that."

She set down her coffee. "It's not consequences. It's a life. In eight months, we'll have a baby. You're either in for the whole messy ride or you're not. If you expect me to believe you're the least bit interested, you're going to have to show a little enthusiasm and energy."

Annoyance tightened his muscles. What the hell did she want from him? Blood? He'd shown up and apologized. And he'd meant it. Every word. He was willing to accept that he was totally in the wrong, that they were having a baby and he wanted to be part of that baby's life.

"This is a big step for me," he said slowly, trying to keep his temper from showing. "I never wanted children, never thought about having them. Suddenly everything is different. I'm doing my best to make the mental shift. Could you give me a break on that? A lot of guys wouldn't have even tried. I deserve some credit for showing up."

She folded her arms over her chest. "Oh my, yes. Big, big points for showing up. Yeah, you. What a fabulous man you are. The great Dr. Josh Daniels showed up. If you'd given me more warning, I could have arranged a band to be playing."

She was furious and should have looked ridiculous in her robe and curlers, yet she didn't. Her words stung enough to make him want to lash out. He knew instinctively that was the road to disaster so he struggled to find a better way to say what he meant.

Before he could, she said, "This is going to get me into trouble, but at this point, I don't actually care. I want the truth, Josh. I don't care if it's pretty. Just go with your gut on this. Are you sure you never wanted children or did you decide that after you met Stacey and found out she couldn't have kids? Was it your decision or a way to make her feel better?"

The question ran into him like a truck. He managed to keep standing and hold in his need to deny the implication of her words. Then he stunned them both by saying, "I don't know."

Crissy stared at him, her eyes wide, her mouth partially open. "I'll give you credit for honesty," she whispered. "I never thought you'd say that."

"Me, either. Too bad about the band not being here. They could break into song."

She winced. "Sorry. I can get a little sarcastic when I'm pissed off. Plus I really miss caffeine."

"I guess."

"Having a baby with me has nothing to do with Stacey," she said. "Did she really expect you not to have a life after she was gone? It's been four years. Aren't you allowed to move on?"

"It's not that simple," he said. The guilt had come on slowly. At first, when Crissy hadn't mattered that much, he hadn't been bothered at all. He's assumed he'd healed. But lately he realized he hadn't moved on as much as he'd thought.

"What makes it simple?" she asked. "Is the whole world supposed to stop because she died? Should I pay for being alive by giving up everything important to me?"

"Of course not."

"Then why should you?"

Interesting question, he thought grimly. Too bad he didn't have an answer.

"Stacey will always be a part of me," he said. "I can't escape that."

"No one wants you to," she told him. "But make her the best part of you, not the worst. You can be so amazing, but then you go down this dark path where you are only allowed to care about your patients. Is it because they're safe? You get close, but not too close? It's less messy than a real relationship?"

He thought about Tommy and all the kids he'd done his damnedest to keep alive. "They're not a part of this discussion," he said, wanting to warn her off before they went to a place that had no point of recovery.

"Why aren't they?" she asked. "You can't be involved with someone and keep pieces of yourself closed off. We can't keep secrets."

He wanted to tell her they weren't involved, except

they were. If nothing else, they were having a baby together.

He stared at her, knowing their connection was stronger than that. She mattered to him and that was the bottom line of the trouble. When Stacey had died, he'd promised them both he would never fall in love again.

"I can't do this," he said, knowing he had to get out of there.

"You're leaving? Just like that? And you accuse *me* of running away."

"You don't understand." She couldn't. She hadn't been through what he had.

"Then explain it to me. Tell me why what doesn't exist anymore and can never come back matters more than what's right in front of you."

"I loved her. I still love her."

"No one says that should stop. But there's a difference between loving her and respecting the life you had together, and burying yourself alive now."

"I'm not—"

Crissy shook her head, interrupting him. "You know what? Forget it. I'm tired of fighting ghosts. I don't know Stacey. I don't know anything about her. Apparently she was pretty special because after four years you'd still rather be dead with her than alive with someone else."

He hated seeing her in pain. "Crissy, I'm sorry."

"Why? You're getting exactly what you want. You can be alone with your memories. I'm the one who's sorry. I have a lousy romantic history. I tend to pick men who aren't capable of being an emotional partner. They were all so seriously flawed that eventually I simply gave up on men altogether. Then I met you. You seemed…perfect."

She dropped her arms to her sides. "Stupid, huh? You're not perfect. You're just a guy. You have the potential to be a partner, but not the emotional will. Ironic, isn't it? You *can* be, but you choose not to be available. It's safer for you to hide than to take a chance."

She gave him a slight smile. "You know what? Things are so screwed up between us, I'm going to tell you exactly what I think. Probably not a good idea, but what the hell. I think one of the reasons you fell in love with Stacey was that she'd been sick. The fact that she was probably not going to live a normal life span meant you didn't have to try so hard. You got to focus on her and the illness and what might or might not happen. It was easier than risking your heart for real."

He'd been with her until the last point. "What the hell makes you think you know anything about me and Stacey?" he demanded. "Because your many successful marriages make you an expert?"

"I'm giving you one opinion," she said. "I'm sure you'll ignore it. But here's the thing. Getting lost in the past is a breeze. The dead have a way of not making demands. The living are a lot more messy. I have expectations, Josh. Complicated, life-changing, interrupting, badly timed expectations. You wouldn't like that. You like your relationships from a distance. You give a hundred percent to your kids. You're practically a god to their parents, but it's in little doses. You're not there when the kids go home. You don't pick up the pieces. You sweep in with the big gesture. That's how it was with Stacey."

"I don't have to listen to this crap," he said, and walked out of the kitchen.

Rage filled him. She didn't know anything about him or Stacey. She was nothing like his late wife. On her best day she couldn't begin to understand the love they'd shared.

"It's not just me," Crissy said as she followed him. "The baby is going to be the same way. Our child is going to expect you to hang in there, no matter what. What are you going to do then? You say you're ready for the responsibility. I'm sure you're thinking you'll do great through anything that goes wrong. I know you're right about that. You're the go-to guy in a crisis. The place you can't deal is where everything is just fine. What are you going to do if nothing's wrong?"

He walked out her front door and crossed to his car. When he'd driven two blocks, he pulled over. The anger was a wild, living animal inside of him. He wanted to lash out at someone, anyone. He wanted to fight and hit and crush. He wanted to destroy. He wanted…

Damn her all to hell. Why couldn't she understand that he was… He was…

The past returned, sucking him in and drawing him down. Stacey had chosen to die at home. She'd asked for hospice care, but Josh had been there for her at the end. He'd known what to do, how to give her the drugs that would ease the excruciating pain.

Those last days had torn him apart as he'd watched

her suffering. She'd hated for him to leave her room, even for a few minutes. She'd needed him so much.

"Promise me you'll love me forever," she whispered, barely able to speak. "You can't love anyone other than me."

"I won't," he'd said, stroking her cheek.

"Not even different," she'd told him. "You can't love someone different and say it's not the same. Promise!"

He'd promised because it had been what he'd believed. How could he ever love again?

But later, while trying to catch a few minutes of sleep in the chair in the corner of her room, he'd thought about her words and wondered why she'd wanted to make sure he couldn't be with anyone else. If he'd been the one dying, he would have wanted her to find happiness, to be in a relationship. Or maybe that was just one of those intellectual arguments. Maybe he couldn't know how it felt to be dying and leaving loved ones behind.

"She wasn't wrong," he said now, aloud in the car. "She wasn't."

He closed his mind to the questions, even as other memories came to him. Their arguments about adopting. How she'd insisted it was wrong to take in a child only to have him or her lose her a few years later. He'd disagreed. She'd always ended their fights by crying that if he loved her he wouldn't talk about it anymore.

He remembered how she always got sick whenever there was something she didn't want to do. How she'd sometimes made it impossible to see Pete and Abbey.

He climbed out of his car and stood by the side of

the road. No! He wasn't going there. Stacey wasn't wrong. She wasn't a bad person. She had been lovely and strong and brave and he'd loved her with an intensity he couldn't possibly match again. She was everything.

She'd also been a bitch on wheels when she didn't get her way.

He swore silently and pushed at the disloyal thought. Stacey was… Not perfect, he admitted to himself. Not evil. Just a person, with good points and flaws.

Not a startling thought, yet one he'd never allowed himself. To him, she'd been an angel in disguise.

But if he made her something she couldn't possibly be, did that rob her of being who she was? His wife. His friend. Someone he would always love. He was grateful she had been in his life. Knowing what he knew now, he would still happily marry her and hope they had forever. But did that mean he had to sacrifice the time he had left because she'd gone first?

He returned to his car and got back inside. Crissy's words echoed around him. He'd thought her expectations, as she'd called them, were unreasonable. Yet weren't they so much less than Stacey had ever asked?

He thought about what Crissy had said about playing it safe. Did he do that? Somewhere along the way had he learned it was better not to lead with his heart? He'd given himself fully to Stacey, but he'd always known their time was limited. He might have told her they could have forty years, but his medical training had known otherwise. She had always been destined to die young.

Had that really been part of her appeal? He hated to think that of himself, but maybe it was true. Crissy was wrong about his commitment to his patients, but there was a possibility she was right about a lot of other things.

His gut had always told him what his mind refused to believe. It had been wrong of Stacey to tell him to never love anyone else. Crissy wouldn't do that to him. She would probably tell him to wait a decent amount of time and to mourn the hell out of her. Then she would tell him to get his ass out there and find someone.

He felt himself smile. Knowing her as he did, she would probably point out that she would be a tough act to follow, but he was welcome to see if someone else could.

Crissy. She'd been a miracle of light in his dark cold world. He knew what she wanted, what she expected, what she needed. Was it possible? Could he do that? Was there a way to reconcile past and present? And if he could find it, did he still have a chance with Crissy or had that bond been broken forever?

"She's beautiful," Crissy said as she held baby Mindy in her arms and stared into big blue eyes. "Possibly the most beautiful little girl ever."

Mindy blinked at her.

"So precious," Crissy whispered, then looked at Noelle who lay on the chaise in her bedroom. "Am I holding her too long? Do you want me to give her back?"

Noelle gave her a weary smile. "I'm so exhausted, I appreciate just lying here. Hold and rock away. I doubt she'll start to cry. She's been really calm."

"It's only been a week," Crissy told the baby. "You're getting so much attention. What is there to cry about?"

Noelle laughed. "You have a point. My mom is staying with me another week. My dad's here every day. Dev's dad is in and out all the time. My sisters adore her, you and Rachel come pretending to visit me but I know you're really here to see the baby. She doesn't have very much to complain about."

Crissy settled in the rocking chair. "What about you? Are you happy?"

Noelle sank back in the cushions and sighed. "I'm past happy—I'm in bliss!"

"Good for you. And Mindy's doing okay, healthwise?"

Noelle and Dev had had a scare during the first few months of Noelle's pregnancy. Further testing had shown that everything was fine with the baby, but until Mindy had been born, neither of them had been totally convinced.

"Her pediatrician says she's thriving. So we've let our worries go. We've been blessed with an amazing baby. Lucky us."

Crissy kissed Mindy's soft cheek. "I agree. Lucky you."

Noelle looked at her. "You're not feeling so lucky. You seem…I don't know. Sad, maybe. Is it Josh?"

Crissy nodded. "We're going to have to agree to disagree on just about everything. I want him to be emotionally engaged—he thinks that would betray his late wife. I want him to be a father who's excited about having a child. He's willing to be responsible and do the right thing."

"Does he need more time?"

"I think he needs a brain transplant." Crissy shook

her head. "I know that's not fair. He's dealing with a lot of things from his past. Honestly I swear Stacey played with his emotions. I feel bad saying it, but I don't think I would have liked her."

"People have different needs at different times," Noelle said.

"Unfortunately I'm pregnant *now*."

"Are you willing to wait for him to come around? Is he worth that?"

"I love him," Crissy said as she rocked the baby. "I can't imagine loving anyone else. So for now, I'll wait. I'm not doing anything else with my time. The thing is, one-sided love isn't looking very good to me these days."

Sunday morning Josh sat on his patio, pretending to read the paper. It was a beautiful day, the kind that made him want to take a hike in the local mountains or drive down to the beach and ride his bike along the boardwalk.

Not by himself, he thought. It would be better to go with someone. Someone like Crissy.

He couldn't stop thinking about her or their last conversation. He'd said everything wrong, done everything wrong. He needed to make things right with her, but didn't know how.

What could he say to explain what he felt when he wasn't sure himself?

Worse than being without her was the fact that he'd hurt her. He'd never wanted that. She was—

He heard a noise and looked up. The bushes by his

patio moved, then Brandon pushed through them and walked toward him, dragging his bike.

Josh couldn't believe his nephew was here. "Tell me you didn't ride your bike here," he told the boy.

Brandon hung his head and shrugged.

Fear clutched at Josh's gut. He was a good five miles from Abbey and Pete's house and there were at least three major streets the kid would have to have crossed.

"Brandon, you're not allowed to leave your neighborhood. You know that. Do your parents know you're gone?"

Still not looking at Josh, he shook his head. "I know I was wrong, but I had to do something." He raised his head. There were tears in his eyes. "I gotta talk to you, Uncle Josh. I tried calling, but someone was always around. Last night I decided to just come here this morning. I know I shouldn't have ridden here all by myself, but it's important."

Josh was furious, but decided not to deal with that right now. He would hear Brandon out, then he would start yelling. But first, there were some worried adults to be taken care of.

"You can leave your bike out here," he said as he led the way inside. He grabbed the phone and dialed a very familiar number. "Abbey, hi. Brandon's with me. And he's fine."

He glared at his nephew as he spoke, assuring Abbey and promising to return her son later that morning. When he hung up, Brandon slumped into a chair.

"I know I'm in trouble," Brandon said, his voice low. "I'm gonna really get it. But I had to."

"I'm ready to hear why."

Brandon looked at him and Josh saw a lot of Crissy in the boy. Her eyes, her mouth. This was her child. What would their child look like? Who would it take after more?

Not the time for those questions, he reminded himself. There were more immediate problems.

"Okay," Brandon began. "But you can't be mad at me."

"About you riding your bike over here?"

"No, about the other stuff."

Josh swore silently. There was other stuff? "I'll save my anger for the end. I'm going to yell at you about riding your bike over here anyway, so we'll get it all done at once. What did you do?"

Brandon sucked in a breath. "I listened when I shouldn't. Last week. I know it's wrong, but it's hard because nobody tells me anything and some of it's really important."

"What did you hear?" Josh asked seconds before the obvious occurred to him. Damn it all to hell did the boy know that—

"Crissy's pregnant." Brandon stared at the kitchen table. "She's gonna have a baby and this time she's going to keep it."

There was a world of confusion and hurt in those words. Josh moved toward his nephew, pulled up another chair and settled in front of him.

"It's weird," Brandon said, still staring at the table. "Crissy's really cool, you know? I like having her around. But is that okay? What about my mom? Does it bother her that I like Crissy? I was trying to figure that out, when I found out about the baby. She's keeping her baby and she didn't keep me. Why, Uncle Josh? Why?"

Josh heard the tears in the boy's voice and pulled him close. Brandon hung on with all his strength as the sobs claimed him.

Josh didn't know what to say to make this child feel better. If only he hadn't heard. The family would have made plans to tell him together. But life was rarely that tidy.

"I love you, kid," he said. "Do you know that?"

Brandon sniffed and nodded.

"Your mom and dad love you."

"I know that," Brandon said impatiently.

"So maybe you'd rather not be their son."

His nephew looked at him in shock and outrage. "What? I'm their son. They love me. I know they love me."

"No one is saying they don't. I was with them when they brought you home. I've never seen any two people so happy. They'd been given the greatest gift of their lives and they knew it."

That earned him a slight smile. "Yeah?"

"Yeah. I'm not saying you don't matter to them, I'm asking if you'd rather they weren't your parents. Would it be better if Crissy had kept you?"

Brandon stared at him, wide-eyed. "No," he breathed. "I like Crissy. I like her a lot, but she's not my mom. I don't want her to be."

"Then you're a lucky guy, because you're going to get exactly what you want. You can stay where you are, have the parents you want and still have Crissy in your life."

Brandon thought about that for a second. "Okay, but the baby… She's keeping him."

"Her life is different. She doesn't know anything about this baby. She's not picking it over you. It's about timing, Brandon. If she'd had a different baby before and she was pregnant with you now, you'd be the one she's keeping."

"Okay," Brandon said slowly. "I kind of understand that."

"Crissy loves you. Giving you up changed her life forever, and not necessarily for the better. She's been missing you since you were born. That's hard."

"I hadn't thought of it that way. So she's been really sad?"

"More than sad." He thought about all she'd said about being unable to be in a relationship. "She didn't want to forgive herself for giving you up. All these years, she's been mad at herself for not being able to give you what you deserved. She's punished herself way more than anyone else would have punished her. Maybe even more than you would have."

"I don't want to punish her," Brandon insisted. "She wasn't bad. She was young and it was hard. Girls shouldn't have babies until they're a lot older."

"Like Crissy's age now?"

"Yeah. Oh." Brandon smiled. "Okay. I get it. She's ready now."

"Yes, she is. It's not about you. Do you understand that?"

He nodded.

Josh pulled him close again. "I'm sorry you overheard that conversation, kid. Not a good way to find out you're going to be a half brother."

Brandon straightened a little. "Half brother? Oh,

yeah. Because Crissy's my birth mom, I'll be related to the baby. That's okay."

"It's a little more complicated that," Josh admitted. "I'm the father."

Brandon jumped to his feet and cheered. "For real? So we're all related. You and me and Crissy and my mom and dad and the girls. It's all of us. That baby is all of us."

"It sure is."

Brandon gave him a high-five. "Totally cool, Uncle Josh. I'm glad you're getting married again. Crissy's the best and if she marries you, she'll always be around."

Married? To Crissy? Josh hadn't thought past the baby being born. Marriage? Love?

"We haven't gotten that far," Josh admitted, stunned by the thought.

"But you have to get married if you're having a baby. Don't you?"

Did they? Marriage. After Stacey, he never thought he would be interested. But then Crissy came along and changed everything.

Brandon grabbed his arm. "Do you love her, Uncle Josh? Because you have to love her. That's the most important thing."

Josh ruffled his hair. "You're a pretty smart kid."

"Smart enough to know you didn't answer the question. Do you love her?"

Josh thought about all he and Crissy had been through. The ways she'd filled his life and brought light to the dark places. How she led with her heart, even though she believed she was tough. How she did the hard thing, because it was right. She was honest and caring, smart and funny, determined, giving. She was the one he'd been waiting for all his life.

"I do love her," he said aloud.

The cemetery was on a hill, with a view of the valley. Stacey had picked the location and the specific spot herself, long before the cancer had returned. At one point she'd teased he could buy the plot for her as a wedding present.

The suggestion had shocked Josh and she'd apologized, but he'd never forgotten. Now, as he walked toward the simple stone that marked her grave, he wondered if they were both guilty of simply waiting for her to die. If each of them had, for different reasons, been unwilling to fully live.

Crissy was right—he'd been afraid to wholly commit. Stacey had given him the perfect out. He could love her unconditionally, knowing time was limited. She wouldn't ask too much of him, because she couldn't.

When she died, he lost himself in mourning. Not only because he had cared about her, but because it was an easy way to avoid a real life.

He walked over the well-kept grass and set flowers by the carved stone. Irises. Her favorite.

He didn't speak. Stacey wasn't in this place. Graves were for the living, not the dead. And he was alive, even if he'd nearly forgotten the truth of that. Alive and desperately in love with a complicated woman who would always expect his best. She might never forgive him for what he'd said. She might refuse to see him.

Either way, he wouldn't stop trying. It was time to start showing up for his life.

Crissy stepped off the treadmill. She was doing her best to run Josh out of her heart. Her doctor said she could run through the first few months with no problem and she intended to take him at his word. If nothing else, she would be in amazing shape by the time the baby was born.

She pulled off her sweatband and grabbed her towel. Sweat dripped off her. She knew she looked like hell—red and damp, with her mascara running—but who cared? She'd designed her gyms for women only. No one here was going to judge her.

She waved at a few members she knew, then crossed to the front of the building, prepared to take the stairs to her office. One of the perks of being the owner was a private bathroom with a shower. She would order in lunch and get back to work. Maybe with her body exhausted, her mind would finally quiet down.

She'd barely taken the first two stairs when she heard someone call her name. A familiar someone. A guy.

Her brain split in two with half of her quivering at the thought of seeing Josh again. It didn't seem to matter that all their conversations were total disasters. She missed him with a desperation that made her wonder if she was ever going to be normal again.

The other half of her brain was aware of how horrible she looked after a ten-mile run. Why did he have to show up now?

She blotted her face with her towel and turned to face

him. The second she saw him her heart gave a lurch, as if calling out to its soul mate.

He looked good, she thought as she studied him. Tired, but handsome. In his jeans and white shirt, he looked sexy enough to be the dessert special of the week.

"I need to talk to you," he said.

She wanted to tell him that this wasn't a good time. She thought about asking him to come back in twenty minutes so she could at least shower. Then she figured she could fight sweaty as easily as she could fight clean.

"We can go to my office," she said, and led the way. It was only when she reached the second floor landing that she realized she never thought to tell him no. That they couldn't talk. Because she was stupid and in love and until she could stop loving him, she would be happy to see him, even if he was a big jerk.

Once behind closed doors, she turned to him. "You have ten minutes, or until you piss me off. Whichever comes first."

"You're packing some attitude this morning," he said. "I like that."

She wanted to tell him she didn't care what he liked, but it wasn't true. She cared too much. She cared to the point of stupid.

"I just ran ten miles. I could kick your ass." She leaned against her desk. "Why are you here?"

"Because being with you is where I belong."

She blinked. What? Had he just said what she thought he— What?

He took a step toward her. "Crissy, I can't find the

words to tell you how sorry I am for what I've put you through. You have been nothing but loving and support-ive and I've sent you to hell and back."

Was this really happening or had she slipped into madness because she loved him so much? Hope grew inside of her. Hope and love and anticipation.

He took her hand in his and stared into her eyes. "You were right about me. About how I've held back and how marrying Stacey made things easier."

"Josh, no," she said. "I was angry and hurt and I lashed out. I'm sorry for what I said."

"Don't be. You told the truth."

"Not about your patients. You give so much to them. You do more than anyone else is willing to. That was a low hit and I apologize."

He touched her face. "How can you be so generous when I hurt you over and over again? Crissy, you ter-rified me. You're so alive and determined. Nothing scares you."

"You're wrong. I'm scared a lot. Brandon terrified me and when I think about having a baby and having to raise it…" She shook her head. "What if I do every-thing wrong?"

"You won't."

"What if my baby hates me?"

"Not possible."

"Let's have this conversation again when he or she is sixteen."

"Teenagers hate everyone."

She smiled. "You're trying to make me feel better. That's nice." More than nice. He'd come to make things better with her. That was worth a lot. Given a little time, maybe he would be willing to open his heart to her.

"I love you," he told her.

"Really?" Apparently he didn't need much time at all. "You mean that? This isn't guilt love?"

He leaned in and kissed her. "Not guilt love at all. Real love. Forever love. The parents of my patients talk about how I'm their miracle. I never got that until now. Because you're my miracle."

Her eyes began to burn, but this time with happy tears.

He kissed her again. "I love you, Crissy. I want to be with you always. I want to fill our house with kids and dogs and laughter and whatever else you want. I want to grow old with you. I want to have a past and a present, with a future we both look forward to. Will you marry me?"

The last of her pain faded as if it had never been. A down-to-the-bone happy contentment filled her. Then a tear slipped down her cheek. "I can't believe you proposed to me when I'm all sweaty."

He grinned. "You look beautiful."

"But I need to take a shower."

The grin broadened. "I could help you with that."

"It's a pretty small shower."

"We can work with it."

Despite the sweat and his clean shirt, she threw herself at him. "I love you, Josh. For always."

"I love you, too. I'm glad we're having a baby. I'm glad I'm having a baby with you. Are you going to make an honest man of me?"

"Yes," she said happily. "I'll marry you. I might even take your name."

"You could hyphenate. Phillips-Daniels. We'll sound very British and aristocratic."

He kissed her. She let herself get lost in the sensation of being close to him. They had time now. Time to deal with things like names and where they would live and whether or not they wanted to know the sex of the baby. They had the rest of their lives. It would be a journey of love. Crissy couldn't wait for it to begin.

* * * * *

*Don't miss the return of bestselling author
Susan Mallery's* DESERT ROGUES *miniseries
to Special Edition.*

Look for
THE SHEIK AND THE CHRISTMAS BRIDE
*On sale November 2007
wherever Silhouette Books are sold.*

And turn the page for a sneak peek at
TEMPTING,
*the new chapter in Susan Mallery's family saga,
coming next month from HQN Books.*

CHAPTER ONE

"LET ME MAKE THIS EASY for you," the man in the expensively tailored suit told Dani Buchanan. "You don't get to speak to the senator until you tell me why you're here."

"Amazingly enough, that information doesn't make things easier," Dani murmured. She'd already talked her way through a receptionist and two assistants. She could actually see Mark Canfield's door just down the hall. But standing between her and it was a big, determined-looking man.

She thought about pushing past him, but he was pretty tall and she wasn't. Not to mention the fact that she'd actually worn a dress and high heels—neither of which were normal for her. The dress was no big deal, but the heels were killing her. She could handle the pain in the balls of her feet and the slight pulling in her arches, but how did anyone stay balanced on these things? If she moved at anything faster than a stroll, she was in danger of snapping an ankle.

"You can trust me," the man said. "I'm a lawyer."

Dani smiled. "A profession designed to inspire trust? I don't think so."

His lips twitched, as if he were holding in a smile. A good sign, she thought. Maybe she could charm her way past this guy. Not that she'd ever been especially good at charming men, but if she could fake it, that would be enough.

She drew in a breath and tossed her head. Of course, her hair was cut short, which meant there was no flip over her shoulder. Which left Dani completely out of charming-men-type tricks. Good thing she'd sworn off dating for the rest of her life.

"Think of me as the dragon at the gate," the man said. "You're not getting past me until I know your business."

"Didn't anyone ever tell you that dragons are extinct?"

Now he did smile. "I'm living proof they're alive and well."

Fine, she thought absently. She would go all the way to fine for this guy. He had a nice face—handsome enough that you wouldn't turn to stone looking at him, but not so pretty that he wouldn't need to develop a personality. Killer blue eyes. A strong jaw, which meant stubborn.

"I'm here for personal reasons," she said, knowing that wasn't going to be enough, but feeling the need to try.

Dragon-man's face tightened as he crossed his arms

over his chest. Dani instantly had the sensation of being shut out and judged, all at the same time.

"I don't think so," the man said sharply. "The senator doesn't play those kind of games. You're wasting your time. Get the hell out of here."

Dani stared at him. "Huh?" What was he… Oh. "You think I'm implying the senator and I—" She grimaced. "Yuck. No! Never. Ew." She took a step back, a dangerous act, considering the shoes, but she had no choice. Distance was required. "That is too disgusting for words."

"Why?"

She sighed. "Because there's a chance I'm his daughter." Better than a chance.

Suit-guy didn't even blink. "You'd do better to imply you were sleeping with him. I'd be more inclined to believe you."

"Who are you to pass judgment on what Mark Canfield may or may not have been doing twenty-nine years ago?"

"I'm his son."

That got his attention. "Alex, I presume?"

Dragon-guy nodded.

Interesting. Not that she and the senator's oldest son were related. Mark Canfield and his wife had adopted all their children, including Alex. But it was possible they were family.

Dani wasn't sure how she felt about that. Dealing with her own family was complicated enough. Did she want to take on another one?

The sense of needing to belong by blood burned hot enough to give her the answer. If Mark Canfield really was her father, she wanted to get to know him, and no one was going to get in her way. Not even his oldest and unrelated-to-her son.

"I've been patient through one secretary and two assistants," she said firmly. "I've been polite and understanding. If nothing else, I'm a registered voter in this state and I have every right to see my senator. Now if you'll just step aside, before I'm forced to escalate the situation."

"Are you threatening me?" Alex asked, sounding almost amused.

"Would it work?" she asked.

He slowly looked her up and down. In the past six months she'd learned that male attention was not a positive thing in her life. It inevitably ended in disaster. But even though she'd sworn off men, she still felt a little quiver as his steady gaze drifted across her body.

"No, but it might be fun," he said.

"You are such a guy."

"Is that a bad thing?"

"You have no idea. Now step aside, dragon-boy. I'm going to see Mr. Canfield."

"Dragon-boy?"

The amused voice hadn't come from the person in front of her. Dani turned toward the sound and saw a familiar man standing in front of an open door.

She recognized Senator Mark Canfield because she'd seen him on television. She'd even voted for him. But those acts had been from a distance. She'd never thought of him as more than a political figure. Now he was here and there was a very good chance he was her father.

She opened her mouth, then closed it. Words faded from her brain as if she'd just lost the power of speech.

The senator walked toward them. "Are you dragon-boy, Alex?" he asked the younger man.

Alex shrugged, looking faintly uncomfortable. "I told her I was the dragon at the gate."

The senator patted his much taller son on the back. "You do a good job, too. So is this young lady a particular threat?" He turned to Dani and smiled. "You don't look especially threatening."

"I'm not," she managed to say.

"Don't be so sure," Alex told him.

Dani glared. "You're being a little judgmental here."

"You're going to make trouble with your ridiculous claims."

"Why are they ridiculous? You don't know for sure, yet."

"Do you?" Alex asked.

The senator looked at both of them. "Should I come back at a better time?"

Dani ignored Alex. "I'm sorry to barge in like this. I've been trying to make an appointment to see you but every time they ask me why, I can't give them the real reason. I…"

The enormity of what she was about to do crashed in on her. How could she just blurt out what she'd been told? That twenty-nine years ago he'd had an affair with her mother and she was the result? He would never believe her. Why would he?

Mark Canfield frowned at her. "You look familiar. Have we met before?"

"Don't even think about it," Alex told her. "You don't want to mess with me."

She ignored him and turned to the senator. "We haven't, but you knew my mother. Marsha Buchanan. I look a little like her. I'm her daughter. And, I think, maybe yours."

* * * * *

THE ROYAL HOUSE OF NIROLI
Always passionate, always proud

The richest royal family in the world—united by
blood and passion, torn apart by deceit and desire.

Nestled in the azure blue of the Mediterranean Sea, the
majestic island of Niroli has prospered for centuries. The
Fierezza men have worn the crown with passion and
pride since ancient times. But now, as the king's health
declines, and his two sons have been tragically killed, the
crown is in jeopardy.

The clock is ticking—a new heir must be found before
the king is forced to abdicate. By royal decree the inter-
nationally scattered members of the Fierezza family are
summoned to claim their destiny. But any person who
takes the throne must do so according to The Rules of
the Royal House of Niroli. Soon secrets and rivalries
emerge as the descendents of this ancient royal line vie
for position and power. Only a true Fierezza can become
ruler—a person dedicated to their country, their people…
and their eternal love!

Each month starting in July 2007,
Harlequin Presents is delighted to bring you
an exciting installment from
THE ROYAL HOUSE OF NIROLI,
in which you can follow the epic search
for the true Nirolian king.
Eight heirs, eight romances, eight fantastic stories!

Here's your chance to enjoy a sneak preview of the
first book delivered to you by royal decree….

FIVE MINUTES LATER she was standing immobile in front of the study's window, her original purpose of coming in forgotten, as she stared in shocked horror at the envelope she was holding. Waves of heat followed by icy chills surged through her body. She could hardly see the address now through her blurred vision, but the crest on its left-hand front corner stood out, the *royal* crest, followed by the address: *HRH Prince Marco of Niroli...*

She didn't hear Marco's key in the apartment door, she didn't even hear him calling out her name. Her shock was so great that nothing could penetrate it. It encased her in a kind of bubble, which only concentrated the torment of what she was suffering and branded it on her brain so that it could never be forgotten. It was only finally pierced by the sudden opening of the study door as Marco walked in.

"Welcome home, *Your Highness*. I suppose I ought to curtsy." She waited, praying that he would laugh and tell her that she had got it all wrong, that the envelope she was holding, addressing him as Prince Marco of Niroli, was some silly mistake. But like a tiny candle flame shivering vulnerably in the dark, her hope trembled fearfully. And then the look in Marco's eyes extinguished it as cruelly as a hand placed callously over a dying person's face to stem their last breath.

"Give that to me," he demanded, taking the envelope from her.

"It's too late, Marco," Emily told him brokenly. "I know the truth now…." She dug her teeth in her lower lip to try to force back her own pain.

"You had no right to go through my desk," Marco shot back at her furiously, full of loathing at being caught off guard and forced into a position in which he was in the wrong, making him determined to find something he could accuse Emily of. "I trusted you…."

Emily could hardly believe what she was hearing. "No, you didn't trust me, Marco, and you didn't trust me because you knew that I couldn't trust you. And you knew that because you're a liar, and liars don't trust people because they know that they themselves cannot be trusted." She not only felt sick, she also felt as though she could hardly breathe. "You are Prince Marco of Niroli…. How could you not tell me who you are and still live with me as intimately as we have lived together?" she demanded brokenly.

"Stop being so ridiculously dramatic," Marco demanded fiercely. "You are making too much of the situation."

"Too much?" Emily almost screamed the words at him. "When were you going to tell me, Marco? Perhaps you just planned to walk away without telling me anything? After all, what do my feelings matter to you?"

"Of course they matter." Marco stopped her sharply. "And it was in part to protect them, and you, that I decided not to inform you when my grandfather first announced that he intended to step down from the throne and hand it on to me."

"To protect me?" Emily nearly choked on her fury. "Hand on the throne? No wonder you told me when you first took me to bed that all you wanted was sex. You *knew* that was the only kind of relationship there could ever be between us! You *knew* that one day you would be Niroli's king. No doubt you are expected to marry a princess. Is she picked out for you already, your *royal* bride?"

* * * * *

Look for
THE FUTURE KING'S PREGNANT MISTRESS
by Penny Jordan in July 2007,
from Harlequin Presents,
available wherever books are sold.

Silhouette®

Romantic
SUSPENSE

Sparked by Danger,
Fueled by Passion.

Mission: Impassioned

A brand-new miniseries begins with

My Spy

By *USA TODAY* bestselling author

Marie Ferrarella

She had to trust him with her life....
It was the most daring mission of Joshua Lazlo's
career: rescuing the prime minister of England's
daughter from a gang of cold-blooded kidnappers.
But nothing prepared the shadowy secret agent
for a fiery woman whose touch ignited something
far more dangerous.

My Spy

#1472

Available July 2007 wherever you buy books!

REQUEST YOUR FREE BOOKS!
2 FREE NOVELS PLUS 2 FREE GIFTS!

SPECIAL EDITION®

Life, Love and Family!

YES! Please send me 2 FREE Silhouette Special Edition® novels and my 2 FREE gifts. After receiving them, if I don't wish to receive any more books, I can return the shipping statement marked "cancel." If I don't cancel, I will receive 6 brand-new novels every month and be billed just $4.24 per book in the U.S., or $4.99 per book in Canada, plus 25¢ shipping and handling per book and applicable taxes, if any*. That's a savings of at least 15% off the cover price! I understand that accepting the 2 free books and gifts places me under no obligation to buy anything. I can always return a shipment and cancel at any time. Even if I never buy another book from Silhouette, the two free books and gifts are mine to keep forever.

235 SDN EEYU 335 SDN EEY6

Name _____ (PLEASE PRINT)

Address _____ Apt. _____

City _____ State/Prov. _____ Zip/Postal Code _____

Signature (if under 18, a parent or guardian must sign)

Mail to the **Silhouette Reader Service™**:
IN U.S.A.: P.O. Box 1867, Buffalo, NY 14240-1867
IN CANADA: P.O. Box 609, Fort Erie, Ontario L2A 5X3

Not valid to current Silhouette Special Edition subscribers.

Want to try two free books from another line?
Call 1-800-873-8635 or visit www.morefreebooks.com.

* Terms and prices subject to change without notice. NY residents add applicable sales tax. Canadian residents will be charged applicable provincial taxes and GST. This offer is limited to one order per household. All orders subject to approval. Credit or debit balances in a customer's account(s) may be offset by any other outstanding balance owed by or to the customer. Please allow 4 to 6 weeks for delivery.

Your Privacy: Silhouette is committed to protecting your privacy. Our Privacy Policy is available online at www.eHarlequin.com or upon request from the Reader Service. From time to time we make our lists of customers available to reputable firms who may have a product or service of interest to you. If you would prefer we not share your name and address, please check here. ☐

n o c t u r n e™

**DON'T MISS THE RIVETING CONCLUSION
TO THE RAINTREE TRILOGY**

RAINTREE: SANCTUARY

by *New York Times* bestselling author

BEVERLY BARTON

Mercy, guardian of the Raintree
homeplace, takes a stand against
the Ansara wizards to battle for
the Clan's future.

*On sale July,
wherever books are sold.*

COMING NEXT MONTH

**#1837 THE MAN WHO HAD EVERYTHING—
Christine Rimmer**
Montana Mavericks: Striking It Rich
When Grant Clifton decided to sell the family ranch, how would he tell Stephanie Julen, the caretaker who'd always been like a little sister to him, that she and her mother would have to leave…especially now that he was head-over-heels in love with her? Was the man who had everything about to lose it all in a betrayal of the woman he was falling for?

#1838 THE PLAYBOY TAKES A WIFE—Crystal Green
As the new CEO of his family's corporation, scandal-sheet regular Lucas Chandler needed an image makeover fast. Visiting a Mexican orphanage seemed like the perfect PR ploy for the playboy—until volunteer and ultimate good girl Alicia Sanchez taught him a lesson in living the good life through good works…and lasting love.

#1839 A BARGAIN CALLED MARRIAGE—Kate Welsh
Her mother's troubled relationships had always cast a pall over Samantha Hopewell's own hunt for Mr. Perfect. Then Italian race-boat driver Niccolo Verdini came to recover from an accident at her family manor, and the healing began…in Samantha's heart.

#1840 HIS BROTHER'S GIFT—Mary J. Forbes
Alaskan bush pilot Will Rubens had carved out a carefree life for himself—until Savanna Stowe showed up on his doorstep with Will's orphaned nephew in tow. Will now found himself the guardian of a young autistic boy…but it was earth mother Savanna who quickly took custody of Will's affections.

#1841 THE RANCHER'S SECOND CHANCE—Nicole Foster
As childhood sweethearts, dirt-poor Rafe Garrett and wealthy Julene Santiago had let their differences tear them apart. Now, years later, Julene returned to town to help her ailing father—and ran smack dab into Rafe. Would the old, unbridgeable gulf reopen between them… or would the love of a lifetime get a second chance?

#1842 THE BABY BIND—Nikki Benjamin
After several unsuccessful attempts at conceiving left her marriage in tatters, Charlotte Fagan had one last hope—to adopt a foreign child. For the application to be approved, though, she and her estranged husband, Sean, would have to pretend to still be together. He agreed to go along with the plan—on one condition….